THE ANIMAL LOOKED UP.

One emerald eye blazed with hatred. The other had been malformed, only a patch of fur where the socket should have been. Forepaws with glistening talons raked the air to hold Ralston at bay.

"Here, over here!" yelled Bernssen, waving his arms and trying to distract the creature.

Ralston saw his chance and acted. The spear flashed forward once more, finding a vulnerable throat. Blood spurting, the creature spun back to face Ralston. He closed the contacts once more. The electrical surge flopped the creature onto its side. It lay there, feebly pawing the air. Bernssen came up, breathing hard, and said, "Never saw anything like it."

"Look at its claws. They're metallic—naturally metallic. And the musculature. Such a powerful creature, but twisted out of shape."

"What spawned such a monster?" asked Bernssen.

"It's a mutant," said Ralston. "A mutant spawned by chaos."

THE WEAPONS OF CHAOS

BOOK 2: EQUATIONS OF CHAOS
ROBERT E. VARDEMAN

ACE BOOKS, NEW YORK

EQUATIONS OF CHAOS

An Ace Book/published by arrangement with
the author

PRINTING HISTORY
Ace edition/July 1987

ISBN: 0-441-87631-5

Ace Books are published by The Berkley Publishing Group,
200 Madison Avenue, New York, N.Y. 10016.
PRINTED IN THE UNITED STATES OF AMERICA

**For Dennis and Lou
and the brainstorming sessions**

ONE

THE RAYS FROM the distant star cast wan shadows but provided no warmth to the planet. Nothing on this darkness-shrouded world had ever tasted the life-giving full warmth of a sun, but still life flourished. No chlorophyll worked its magic inside plants. Photosynthesis provided a curiosity for the laboratory, an intriguing speculation more philosophical than empirical or useful. No DNA dictated the patterns of life on the frigid world. But life did exist.

From the planet's inner fires came the spark for life, and because of a mindless tenacity that knew no bounds, the life forms not only grew, but flourished in this dark, freezing environment.

Beq slithered toward a pillar of warmth and wrapped long, wispy tendrils about the column of dark, razor-edged lava. The creature gave a sigh and snuggled closer, replenishing its energy, thanking the All Wise for providing such a fine dinner. After a decent pause, Beq reluctantly pulled free of the pillar and flowed on its way. As much as it wished to dawdle, the war effort required uncharacteristically swift motion and decisive action. Beq's tendrils elongated even more when a frigid gust blew past.

Liquid ammonia winds caught the tenuous body and lofted it. Beq sighed again, relishing the cold as much as it had the warmth of its energy meal. Each presented differ-

1

ent stimuli, a commodity sadly lacking on such a barren home world.

Beq felt itself carried along faster and faster, until its body resembled a spider web caught in a hurricane. Consciousness began to fade as the body dissipated. Beq vaguely sensed the problem and pulled the vagrant body parts inward until a reasonable level of thought could be maintained. Beq, as did so many others of its spawn-time, enjoyed the peaceful nothingness of being pulled into vapor. The world leaders, however, discouraged such rash, dangerous activity in the younger generations.

The war required full effort. Everyone had to be coherent if the enemy was to be defeated.

But Beq had never seen the enemy. There had never been any attacks on the world. The same lava columns of its youth still provided sustenance. The ammonia winds still blew. Only the intense focusing of the entire planet's meager resources marked any noticeable change in policy over the past years.

Beq coalesced into a tight sphere, presented more resistance to the ammonia plumes, and fell heavily to the rocky surface. Body reforming into a new motile shape, it slithered into a tiny crevice. Volcanic warmth thrilled it once again. The only benefit Beq saw from this elusive war lay in frequent visits to the seat of power on the planet. The ruling committee always chose the most energetic spots for their meetings. And why not? Beq approved of the increased alertness in such surroundings. If the world had to be at war, why shouldn't some of the inhabitants enjoy heightened awareness?

Beq always reveled at the feel of warmth oozing through its body and bringing mentation to a higher level.

The creature sighed. Those higher planes of awareness always brought ineffable emotions, too. Beq preferred floating mindlessly on the winds until its energy level sank almost to death. But as the ruling committee decreed, each must contribute to the effort.

Beq contributed more than most, being the outstanding theoretical mathematician of its spawn-time.

"Report," came the crisp command from the creature chosen this day to head the ruling committee.

Another, clutching at a steamy lava rock, reluctantly freed itself and descended to the center of the chamber. "There is progress in our effort," the being stated in an overly theatrical manner.

Beq allowed its tendrils to snake forth and lightly brush several warm rocks. Energy flowed into its main body and elevated thought processes to the point where it saw truth and knew this creature lied. "Why do you say this?" Beq demanded. "What setbacks have there been for you to hide it so?"

The creature assumed a defensive form. "The enemy has destroyed every weapon we sent this past time increment."

To Beq this meant little. Time flowed in spurts, and often took on a fugue state where the universe halted. The ruling committee had been waging this war for . . . how long? Beq had no easy answer to this, nor did it matter. Its realm was almost entirely theoretical, and Beq experienced its greatest uneasiness and feelings of impatience when dealing with substantive events.

"What was the nature of our weapon? How was it destroyed?" Beq showed uncharacteristic impatience. Although it enjoyed the warmth, it preferred to spend time as it chose. The ruling committee insisted on these meetings every hundred revolutions of the star.

"The method of destruction is unknown. Our weapon induced a field that would disrupt the enemy's cellular structure."

"How odd," Beq said.

The being presiding interrupted. "The enemy is of a fixed form, comprised of living cells that use chemical energy rather than radiation, as is normal."

"How truly odd," Beq said. It had not known that the enemy's form differed so radically. It tightened tendrils around several black, craggy upjuts. The warmth heightened Beq's senses.

"You develop new thoughts?" demanded another on the ruling committee. "We must hear these ideas immediately."

Beq sighed. Such impatience would be their downfall. But it appreciated the ruling committee's dilemma. The war had raged for too long. These pesky enemy creatures did whatever it was they did, and annoyed everyone. To see so many of its spawn-time occupied with war tasks, provoked sympathy and even sorrow in Beq.

"I have been studying," Beq said. "The methods used for our attack are of an obvious nature. The enemy expects and counters such weapons with ease."

A creature elsewhere in the chamber snorted derisively at this. Beq ignored it.

"A more fundamental attack is required, one that the enemy will not understand and respond to." Beq gushed forth and assumed the central spot, so that all on the ruling committee might see it. Beq cared little for such attention but found it necessary if this war was to be ended. So many *interesting* questions remained unanswered. The war only absorbed energy better spent contemplating important problems.

"As the winds carried my body," Beq went on, "mathematical formulations came to me. And a question. Are the ammonia currents truly random?"

"Of course not," scoffed one of the ruling committee. "We have long since derived the physics of their motion. Uneven heating of the surface, mass differentials, the action of gravity, convection, all these play a role in causing the winds to blow."

"This is my thought," agreed Beq. "To know every variable, to place this data into the appropriate thermodynamic equation, add the differential equations of molecular motion, and we might know precisely the path of the winds." Beq paused to absorb more energy. "But the slightest deviation radically alters those state equations.

The most minute fluctuation alters the outcome of our most precise predictions."

"You speak of quantum mechanical fluctuations?"

"Grosser ones. The cracking of a rock. The passage of a cloud between star and surface. The wing motion of a single insect. These are adequate to turn an ordered system into chaos."

Another creature snorted derisively at Beq's idea. "An insect wing turns a breeze into a gale? Ridiculous."

"So?" Beq began a careful explanation of the set of coupled nonlinear differential equations it had derived while floating on the cold winds. For several slow planetary rotations it revealed all that had come to mind during the times of deliberate, slow, penetratingly precise thought.

"You can describe randomness," concluded one of the ruling committee. "But of what use is this to the war effort?"

"The enemy sensors are acute. They detect our most carefully shielded weapons." Beq waited for disagreement. None came. "I propose a weapon that is not a weapon. A field of disorder can be constructed and sent toward the enemy home planet."

It began sketching out the salient points of its plan. A full revolution of the planet around the distant star passed before Beq's mathematical proposal had been presented.

"This field will then confuse their bodies?" asked one of the ruling committee.

This garnered only scorn from its more attentive and astute colleagues. Beq had presented the material clearly and concisely. The creature only showed its lack of concentration and low energy level by such a query.

"It disrupts the most basic processes, not only in life, but of other physical events," Beq explained patiently. "Their chemical processes might take odd turns, some reactions proceeding normally while others produce random events. Weather patterns on their planet would shift. The physical movement of electrons would be disrupted, causing neural damage in their brains and malfunction in their equipment.'' Beq sighed. It seemed a perversion of a fine theory to use it in such a fashion.

"How did you happen to come upon this system of equations?"

Beq sighed once more. Tiny currents of ammonia drifted away from it. "I considered how inefficient it was to wait for thermal activity to rise to the surface for our consumption. The equations for predicting radioactive decay linked into those of chaos.''

"You can create radiation?" The creature shifted about a large lava rock spire. The others of the ruling committee moved away from it. Such a display of ignorance reflected badly on all their number.

"There are many forms of radiation," said Beq. "I wanted to predict—and create—radioactive decay. These equations suggest a way of causing any substance to become radioactive. Even lead." Beq found itself lost in the labyrinth of wondrously complex equations. A cold gust of ammonia along one tendril brought it back to the necessity of speaking with the ruling committee.

"This will bring us much warmth for many years," said a committee member. "But your true accomplishment will be in the creation of a weapon to destroy our enemy. Their sensitive electronic sensing equipment will fail. Their planet becomes uninhabitable due to action of wind and wave. Their very bodies will rebel against them when their brains no longer produce reliable neural connections. Your name, Beq, will be revered throughout our long history.''

Beq barely heard. Already, it followed different pathways through the multiple solutions to the chaos equations. They danced into imaginary realms and back into the physical world. Warmth! No longer dependent on the slow march of heat from the world's magma-laden center, Beq could generate more potent radiation for warming the body.

Beq sobered as it considered the ramifications. What would this do to society? If all had an abundant source of energy, would this destroy the simple pleasures? To never again drift almost comatose on the ammonia winds, because the whole surface glowed with energy, robbed all of a valuable intellectual retreat. Beq's finest ideas came when tendrils were cast forth and the gusty winds lofted its body in an aimless fashion. Thoughts barely possible, all contact with body gone, Beq managed its finest theoretical work in this desultory state.

It would vanish if it allowed unlimited generation of radioactive sources. The others, especially those of the ruling committee, showed such greed for energy. They weren't like Beq, who appreciated aloneness and an opportunity to meditate deeply.

Beq sighed. Its discovery of the equations governing randomness couldn't be hidden. Another would derive the necessary matrices, given a rotation or a revolution or a thousand. Beq had to content itself with the notion that the enemy would at last be removed, allowing everything to return to normal.

Compassion did not enter Beq's consciousness. Such an emotion had to be reserved for only the highest energy state. But Beq came close. To destroy another civilization with such an awesome—and awful—chaos field, bothered it.

But not for long. Beq found a weakly rising thermal, distended its body, and caught the feathery extensions on the ammonia as it evaporated and mingled with the atmosphere.

The chaos weapon had no substance. The mechanicians overseeing its construction worked with tools that were more theoretical than physical. But this disturbed none of them. Beq drifted nearby, thoughts on the equations holding the field in place. With the senses the creature possessed, it saw only blackness against blackness, an occluding rather than a hole. But Beq knew the field quivered with vibrant energy. Every oscillation caused Beq to shudder, as it disturbed the very fabric of both living body and inanimate matter.

"Are you finished?" Beq asked of the mechanicians.

Neither of the creatures attained a high enough energy level to be disturbed by the restrained chaos. Their bodies shimmered and distended with every pulsation in the randomness, but their minds were untouched. Beq wished it could attain that level and let itself drift aimlessly on the ammonia winds.

But now, with its knowledge of the chaos equations, nothing could ever prove truly random for it. Beq could calculate, solve, know. Such power robbed it of speculation about the universe.

Beq tightened and rolled over on the ground, sensory apparatus studying the planetary surface. Since they had allowed the chaos field to come into existence, the weather patterns had grown unstable. The ammonia thermals it so loved to ride had vanished, replaced with violent storm winds which ripped drifting tendrils asunder. Beq had cautioned the ruling committee about allowing the chaos field to come into existence on the surface; it had requested some point in space.

The vote had gone against Beq. The ruling committee felt that secrecy outweighed any danger to their planet. Even when Beq presented the equations governing the randomness and showed potential effects, the ruling committe had insisted. Beq had not argued. To do so would waste precious energy.

Even though the black-on-black field disrupted the planet, Beq felt a high energy surge of love for it. Seldom did any of its race see their theoretical, highly abstruse thoughts turned into something physical. Beq's chaos equations had proven themselves worthy of the highest praise. Mathematics bloomed into reality.

Beq curled a dozen tendrils around a pillar of fiercely radiating lead and allowed its energy level to soar. One of the first applications it had insisted on was the transmutation of inert substances into radioactive ones. The mere presence of the chaos field had worked its randomness on the particles within the lead atoms. Quantum level transitions took place more often than those from uranium, and provided energy for detailed thought.

"Beq, we must hurry. One of the enemy weapons approaches our planet. This device must halt the progress."

Beq curled into a tight sphere, then extended pseudopods to turn and face the member of the ruling committee. "What is the nature of their weapon?" it asked.

The ruling committee member rippled. "It is another of their puzzle weapons." Beq worked on understanding this statement. Their enemy, like them, fought not with explosives and nuclear devices, but with conceptual weapons. One such weapon had jumbled thought processes, but nothing more. Still another had blanked light from the distant star.

Beq had worried over this. Why had the enemy considered this a weapon? Beq had decided that enemy reconnaissance and intelligence had been faulty—or ethnocentric. Beq found it difficult to believe that any intelligent race could survive off chemical energy derived indirectly from sunlight; curling up around a rock post and absorbing the radiant warmth seemed much more direct and efficient. But if the enemy had the same trouble understanding, it made a twisted sort of sense that they might blank out the sunlight, thinking this would cripple those on the planet.

The ruling committee hadn't even noticed the attack for over three revolutions around the primary. One theoretical astronomer had commented that verifying its spectroscopic theories had become difficult. Only then had anyone become concerned.

"This weapon will tear at the fabric of space," declared the ruling committee member.

Beq sighed. Such drama ought to be reserved for the theatre. The chaos field performed according to the abstract equations Beq had derived and implemented. This weapon was a mathematical construct and nothing more. Beq predicted random events with the system of equations, then used conformal mappings of those same equations to cause the event they predicted.

"The field will disrupt their weapon, no matter what it is," said Beq. "I have chosen carefully the sets of equations governing this device. The nuclear adhesion force will weaken. We might be flooded with a radiant shower of leptons and baryons as their weapon comes apart, but this will be a minor event."

Inflicting intense uncertainty on the nuclear force appealed to Beq's intellectual curiosity. It wondered if the weaker forces might likewise be manipulated. To disrupt gravity, such a weak force, might allow indefinite soaring on even the most meager of breezes. Beq worked through the potential before it. Total removal of gravity would not do. It still needed convection currents for the proper lift and sensuous feel of moving cool vapor along its tendrils. But a major diminution in gravity might prove exciting, if in the proper low energy state.

Beq supervised the launching in the field, if launching was the proper word. The chaos field lacked extension, and retained existence only in abstract manner. The mechanicians maneuvered it about, using Beq's instructions, manipulating probability of the field's location. The blackness vanished in one spot, only to *be* in another. No distance seemed to be traversed. This didn't upset Beq. It had no clear idea as to the complete properties of the chaos field it had brought into this war. Beq merely observed and correlated. Later, on its wondrous thermals, energy levels sinking and mind operating at almost animalistic levels, Beq would consider all this.

"Allow it to meet the enemy weapon," Beq ordered. A shimmer of excitement passed through the thin tendrils wrapped about the pillar of radioactive lead. Beq forced itself to ever higher energy levels, straining to observe, keeping its mind on the chaos field.

The weapon vanished, leaving behind only dust.

"Stop!" barked Beq, halting a mechanician as it slid toward the launch area. "Be careful. My calculations show release of the binding energy for quarks in the planetary surface. There is no information on such radiation's effects."

The member of the ruling committee waved away the slowly drifting mechanicians. The entire rocky plain would be cordoned off until counteracting abstractions could be brought to erase the residual chaotic effects.

"There is little time before the enemy realizes something has gone awry with their weapon," said Beq. It floated just above the surface, mind turned to geometries of ever higher orders. These tensors thrilled Beq more than the chaos equations now. It had mastered one complex set of equations. Unless it wanted to risk boredom, it had to seek new diversions.

"Our orbiting sensors relay the battle at forty planetary diameters," said the member of the ruling committee. "The chaos field interacted with their puzzle weapon."

"So?" prompted Beq. The only thing it disliked more than the officiousness of the ruling committee was their strained sense of the dramatic.

"The fields mingled."

"An inexact phrase," murmured Beq. It drifted on a vagrant breeze of cool ammonia, wanting to be free of the ruling committee and this inexplicable war.

Beq allowed a few moments thought to cover the history of the conflict. It found no reason for it. The chemical burners had no interest in Beq's home; why should they? Paradise to one was purgatory to another. Beq found it impossible to believe the enemy, with its precise, ugly form and inefficient internal chemical combustion, would want to populate this world or live under rules of polite society formulated ten million years earlier. The ruling committee did not often allow more than carefully done thought experiments to be performed, unless some more physical tool was required for survival.

This suited Beq. Nothing aroused it so much as the solitude and lowered energy levels where it returned to a bestial state. Its best ideas developed unhindered by the coils of polite behavior in such a drifting, floating, soaring existence. But the war?

Beq found no purpose for it.

"The chaos field has disrupted the enemy weapon," said the ruling committee member. "It veers away from our home world."

"And the chaos field itself? What of it?" demanded Beq. A quick mental calculation had produced indeterminacy. The thought of the field returning to the planet meant disaster now that it had been launched. Beq held some curiosity about the chaos field's effect, but not enough to pursue it actively.

"It spins off through the void. Other mathematicians plot its trajectory. Do you wish to—"

"I wish nothing more to do with it," Beq stated flatly. "I find amusement now in higher geometries. The tensors deform strangely near the chaos field. It is puzzling and bears more examination." Beq exhaled strongly, lifted on an ammonia current, and blew toward the plain where the chaos field had been brought into existence.

Beq ignored the strangeness within its body. Residuals in the mathematical sense, it decided. Faint tuggings left from proximity to the chaos device. Nothing of importance. Beq slipped through the atmosphere and allowed its energy level to dip. New and dazzlingly complex geometries assaulted its brain and pleased it mightily.

The chaos device destroyed the enemy weapon, deflected from the puzzle field, and sailed off across the galaxy, leaving confusion and enforced randomness in its wake.

TWO

MICHAEL RALSTON LEANED back in his chair, letting the pneumatic cushion sigh as it worked to shift and adequately cradle his spine. Strong, stubby work-hardened fingers laced behind his dark-haired head and cold gray eyes, which were fixed on the student shifting nervously in front of the archaeology professor's desk.

"Verd, Dr. Ralston," the student said, eyes averted. "That's what I heard."

"Why are you telling me this, Citizen? There's nothing in it for you, is there?" His tone cut like a stainless steel blade. He was growing tired of the campus politics with its Machiavellian turnings and alliances and enmities.

"Doctor!" The student stiffened angrily. "I don't like the way they're convicting you without a hearing."

Ralston turned slightly and idly drummed fingers over his computer console. Set between two large stacks of dusty books, the palely glowing screen seemed out of place. Nowhere else on the campus of the University of Ilium did books appear the norm and the consoles unusual. Two walls of Ralston's tiny office were lined with books, while the large window in the outer wall had been cycled to total transmission, giving the impression of not existing at all. It wasn't unusual for dedicated archaeology students to come into his office and begin to sneeze from the

13

accumulated dust. But Ralston had long since decided this was a fitting, if minor, lesson for any would-be archaeologist to learn.

Ralston didn't mind the jibes of "grave robber." That ancient epithet came into the profession and could even be tolerated with an air of amused superiority. But since he had returned from Alpha 3 with the intricate and potentially profitable alien technology that allowed telepathic transference of information, many on campus had begun calling him something more—and much worse.

"I see by your record, Citizen Karolli, that you're not much of a student. Is it possible you are currying favor with me by making this allegation?"

"I'm sorry I bothered you, Dr. Ralston." The student turned and started to leave. The lock on the door barred his way. "May I leave?" Karolli's hand nervously jiggled the door handle.

"In a moment." Ralston studied the student, wondering who had sent him. Considering the number of enemies Ralston had made since coming to Ilium, it might be any of them. In his younger days—not that long past—Ralston had fought in the Nex-P'torra war on the side of the reptilian Nex. He had seen how the humanoid P'torra had depopulated a half-dozen worlds with their biologic weapons, and had known instantly that such evil had to be opposed.

His stand had proven increasingly unpopular because of clever P'torra agitation on campus, relying on shape prejudices and the malleability of student opinions. The war was over some years back, but the P'torra carried it on, not with planet-shaking bombs and diabolical mutated viruses, but with propaganda. Ralston had seen a P'torra exchange student with his emotion gauging "impulse driver" at the periphery of more than one campus demonstration. The P'torra never overtly agitated. Their method was to direct from the sidelines, using the impulse driver to calculate the precise words, the proper tones, the correct images needed to whip a crowd to a frenzy.

Ralston had been the target of that psychological technology more than once because of his pro-Nex stand.

Karolli might be a P'torra pawn. Or he might represent more human but nonetheless inimical factions. The newly promoted Chancellor of the University had no love for Ralston. Dr. Salazar's animosity ran deep and knew no bounds. But Ralston didn't fear Salazar, not in the same way he did the P'torra. Academic infighting had always proved non-lethal, as far as life went. Ralston's tenure might be denied again, he might find it impossible to get research grants, he might be passed over for the choicest of the archaeological finds, he might even be evicted from his small, dusty office, but no physical harm would come from that.

Or were there other players in the game? Ralston sighed. Life had been much simpler, if less intellectually stimulating, before he had discovered the ruins on Alpha 3 and returned to Novo Terra and the University with the telepathic projector.

"You," Ralston said, "might be sincere. I'll operate on that assumption. What is it you want me to do about this threat against my continued good health?"

The student shrugged. "Just thought you should know what's being said."

"Where did you hear it?" The way Karolli blanched when Ralston asked, told the archaeology professor a great deal. And he didn't like it. From Karolli's records, Ralston had made a good guess as to the source. Another player *had* entered the game, and this one held power far beyond that of Chancellor Salazar or even the P'torra with his impulse driver and eager throngs of students.

"I . . . I just heard."

"From the Archbishop?" Ralston asked in a low voice. "Is he telling everyone that I'm tainted with evil, that Satan's imprint must linger on my forehead because I dig up ruins on other worlds?" Ralston saw that his guess hit the mark. He didn't need to detain Citizen Karolli any further. Ralston touched the button under the edge of his desk. A tiny click signaled the lock opening. The student bolted, and almost ran from the small office.

Ralston made certain the door had locked once more, then turned and hiked his feet to the windowsill. He, virtually alone in the entire department, had a glass window looking out over the central University quadrangle. The others preferred programmed pictures, scenes of distant worlds or of snow or oceans or of selected people. Ralston preferred the unplanned parade of students rushing to and fro, some on their way to class. That the University demanded their physical presence instead of viewing through computer screens, made the University of Ilium almost unique.

Ralston preferred it; this was one reason he'd chosen to come to Ilium as a professor. The personal contact meant more to him than having a thousand unseen, nameless, intermittently faceless students getting high grades. But he knew the winds of change blew constantly, even in such a conservative setting. Fewer and fewer classes required physical attendance. Some professors held out for lab courses to be held in central locations, but even their voices were drowned out by the convenience of remote classing, as they called it.

Lack of personal contact, Ralston called it.

"I *like* windows," Ralston said forcefully. And, he silently admitted to himself, he liked teaching. No matter what it became, how it mutated, he liked it.

But with the Archbishop leading the pack of hungry dogs nipping at his heels, what chance did he have? Salazar could put him into academic limbo. The Archbishop might consign him to a Hell of a more than spiritual nature.

Ralston had left behind the Earth of his childhood. Its northern temperate zones had been scorched by nuclear weapons, but civilization had hung on with grim tenacity. That the southern hemisphere remained virtually untouched had been a miracle—one the Church had played on heavily.

Ralston didn't waste time thinking about such things. That much of the Earth had survived seemed sufficient.

That war might never happen again was the miracle. But the hold of Churchmen spread from New Rome in Argentina and now brushed across Ralston.

They had held a convocation and deemed the Alpha 3 technology the work of Satan. Michael Ralston had publicly ridiculed such a notion, and drawn their notice and ire. Was Karolli the harbinger of damnation from the Archbishop? Ralston might find himself excommunicated at any instant for his temerity in opposing Church dictates.

Ralston shrugged it off. He preferred to sit and observe the students on the lovely campus Quad stretched out for his unique pleasure. No video display could ever replace the actual substance, depth, and feel of the real scene.

Mind turning to other topics, Ralston jumped when his door alarm sounded loudly. He turned in his chair and touched the key on his console.

"What is it?" he demanded harshly, thinking Karolli had returned with some further tidbit of gossip.

"Sorry to interrupt, Michael," came Leonore Disa's soft voice. "I can come back later."

"Come in." Ralston pressed the button to release the lock. When he'd insisted that one of his students wire the office, the student had laughed. No one but Ralston would request a lock operated independently of the computer. Through the main console any entry and exit could be checked by both the office's occupant and the campus security force. The student had told his professor that this would be convenient in case anyone broke in.

Ralston didn't care to have any illicit office intrusion in the main campus computer's memory, any more than he did his own comings and goings.

Leonore Disa came in and stood in front of his desk, nervously shifting from one foot to the other. It seemed that this was his day to discomfit students. He motioned for the small, dark woman to sit down in the only other chair in the cramped room. She perched on the edge, as if relaxing might be painful. Her surgically implanted jewelry plates had been reprogrammed, Ralston noted. The usual pastels had given way to more garish reds and blues, which highlighted Leonore's cheekbones and gave her a slightly menacing aspect.

He started to comment on this, then bit back the words. He didn't want to get the woman any more upset than she obviously was. Leonore and he had made the discovery on Alpha 3 that led to the alien projector being returned to Novo Terra.

"How's Nels?" he asked, inquiring after Leonore's lover. Nels Bernssen had presented a seminar on pre-nova conditions in stars, which had been well received in the astronomical community.

"He's all right. The talk went well," she said. Her brown eyes fixed on his cooler gray ones. "What are you doing, Michael?" Leonore asked bluntly.

"Not much," Ralston said. "Not much I can do. Salazar took the projector away from me and gave it to the engineering department. That doesn't matter, though, since I'm an archaeologist, not an engineer. With Alpha 3 gone up in the puff of smoke that made Nels' career, there's not much left for me."

"You never struck me as the suicidal type before. Good day, Dr. Ralston." Leonore spun lithely from the chair and almost gained the hallway before Ralston's finger touched the lock button and denied the woman exit.

"I'm not suicidal," he said. "But there's not much I can do right now about the find. Salazar hasn't assigned me a new teaching schedule. He might not next term, either. I'm a consultant, he says." Ralston snorted derisively. "More likely, this is his way of keeping me out of sight."

"To hell with Salazar!" raged Leonore. She slammed both palms flat on his desk and leaned forward, anger accentuated by the bright crimson of her intensely flashing jewelry plates. "So you lost Alpha 3 to the nova. So what?"

"The greatest discovery of this or any other century," sighed Ralston. "Gone in the wavefront from the nova."

"That sun wasn't the right class to go nova," she said.

"Nels is making quite a reputation based on that observation," admitted Ralston.

"And you know why the star blew up. You know why civilization on Alpha 3 declined so suddenly. You know! And you're not doing a damned thing about it!"

"No research money," Ralston said.

"You went back to Alpha 3 without Salazar's approval. You had the confidence in your instincts and you made him buy it. You *forced* him to. If he hadn't agreed that the funding came from the University, my father would have taken it all, telepathic projector included."

Ralston nodded. As it was, Leonid Disa, Leonore's father and chief executive officer of Interstellar Computronics, had claimed marketing rights to the projector. Both the University and IC stood to make billions off the device. Not even the Vegan spider-steel find a decade earlier had netted this much. Ralston decried the way research groups so eagerly sought and exploited the commercial finds, but he knew that he stood alone on this point. The money had to come from somewhere. Only the potential for big returns off alien ruins justified spending the grant money, or so thought the people controlling the funds.

He shook his head as he considered an historical parallel. Spain had pillaged the New World back on Earth, robbing the Incas, Aztecs, and Mayas to fill royal coffers. Yet it had been that plunder that fueled new exploration.

"Whatever happened to pure research?" he muttered.

"Daddy is willing to finance another expedition for you."

"Alpha 3's gone. Poof!" Ralston made an exploding gesture with his hands.

"You learned a great deal from that diorama we brought back. You were locked within it for hours." Leonore relaxed now, settling once more into the chair. But her brown eyes burned with almost religious fervor. Ralston wondered if this was the way he looked when starting on a new dig. Probably.

"The diorama held a great deal of information," he said carefully. "I maintained the telepathic projection alignment by staying within the scene while you and Nels moved it on board the starship." Ralston heaved a deep sigh. While within the alien scene, he had done more than experience the thoughts of the creatures depicted. He had become a part of a history lesson, an active participant complete with all the knowledge held by that creature. The thoughts, emotions, needs, drives, and ambitions—he understood them all while locked within the telepathic projector's invisible grip.

And Michael Ralston knew more than any other human about the last days of civilization on Alpha 3—and how one of the alien scientists, Dial, had labored to save a small number of colleagues from the deadly, lingering effects of the chaos device that had passed by Alpha 3 two hundred years earlier.

"We are in as much danger as those on Alpha 3," Leonore said. Whoever had programmed her jewelry plates had added a skin temperature sensor. As her passion mounted, the colors flashing just under her skin muted and changed. Ralston found himself more interested in this phenomenon than in pursuing the path of the chaos device through space.

"You know where it went. You know where it came from. We can find it!" the woman cried.

Ralston held back a rising tide of emotion. He wanted to tell Leonore that he valued her as a researcher, that her skills would lead her into prominence in archaeology one day. But how could he also tell her that he didn't want her tainted by his increasingly unsavory reputation? Everyone worked against him because he lacked the desire—or the disposition—to play campus politics.

Chancellor Salazar opposed him and denied every tenure vote. The P'torra stirred up student activists against him because of his alliance with and sympathy for the

Nex. Now even the Archbishop of Ilium found reason to publicly denounce him. Ralston *would* follow that device; he *would* learn its secrets; he *would* learn all he could about the race that fashioned such a horrendous weapon. But he didn't want to involve Leonore Disa.

That might end her burgeoning career.

"There's nothing much I can do," he said finally. "I need the money and—"

"My father will supply it—IC will. The chance for a repeat of the telepathic projector sways even the most flint-hearted of IC's miserly directors."

"What use would they put the chaos device to, if I happen to discover it and return with it?" he asked, genuinely curious. "We've seen its effects. It makes otherwise stable stars go nova. It causes epileptic seizures in humans. There's evidence that it creates computer equipment failures. I suppose it might be useful in manufacturing radioactive elements out of those not usually energetic, but . . ." He let his words trail off. Why did IC want to fund what seemed, even to him, a fool's errand?

"The mathematics of it intrigues Daddy," Leonore said. Ralston saw her expression change and become neutral, as if she'd started gambling and didn't want an opponent to know the cards she held. "He says IC can use it for societal predictions."

Ralston leaned back in his chair, his mind racing, trying to put aside his uneasiness that anyone, especially Leonore, might think of the cold, hard Leonid Disa as "Daddy."

"You mean he thinks IC can predict wars if they understand the equations governing the device?" The archaeology professor started to ask what use this might be, then went cold inside when the understanding dawned like a polar morning.

"No one ever accused Daddy of being a pleasant man," Leonore said, a touch of bleakness in her voice. "If the instabilities in a planet's culture that lead to war can be studied and known in advance, vast fortunes can be made."

"Supplying both sides the weapons of war," said Ralston.

"Oh, more than that." Leonore Disa swallowed hard. "Daddy believes it'd be possible to stockpile raw materials that might be in short supply. To know the most likely spots where destruction would occur gives any company an advantage, too. You don't build plants where a bomb will fall."

"And I thought I was a cynical son of a bitch." Ralston shook his head. He felt out of his league. "All I want to do is my research. Let me teach, let me get into the field to study dead civilizations. Is that so much to ask?"

"It is when you make a discovery like this projector. The security forces are already thinking of it as a propaganda device at worst and a brainwashing machine at best."

"I ought to blow up the engineering lab." Desolation washed over Ralston. He hadn't even thought of such applications. For education, for correcting mental disorders—those things he considered for the telepathic projector.

"They've moved it." Leonore saw his expression and hastily added, "I don't know where. I didn't ask, and Daddy wouldn't have told me. It's a joint project now, the University and Interstellar Computronics."

"I can't accept IC's funding for any such expedition. I think you understand why."

"You," said Leonore, "don't want me going along because you think it'd hurt my career."

"It would."

Leonore smiled, tenseness gone. Ralston believed he saw genuine emotion, not an act. "Thank you. I truly appreciate your concern. There aren't many who'd worry over things like that."

"Nels would."

"Yes."

For a few minutes they sat and said nothing. Ralston finally broke the silence. "This is too momentous a discovery for any single private company. I'm not sure I'd even want the government in control of the chaos device."

"Now that they know such a thing is possible, how long

will it be before someone stumbles across it on their own?"

"Nature is a blabbermouth," he admitted. "But it's possible that such work might take years, even centuries. That's beyond me. All I know how to do is poke around in ruins and hunt for garbage and anything else discarded by the people who lived there."

"Michael," she said solemnly, "you're more than that." Leonore rose. "Daddy is a bastard, but he's an honest one. Whatever contract you sign with him, he'll honor. I think it's important to find that machine, or whatever it is, and see if it's still functioning. It might be dangerous to all of us if it is."

Ralston pushed the lock button and opened the door for her. "It passed Alpha 3 more than ten thousand years ago. That's quite a while ago."

Leonore nodded, but he read her thoughts perfectly: Not such a long time, astronomically speaking. The small woman left Ralston to his own musings.

He rocked back and forth in his chair, then launched himself and walked briskly from the office. He'd sat and thought long enough. Accepting Interstellar Computronic's offer to fund an expedition was out of the question. He'd never agree to be in Leonid Disa's debt. He had seen the man and the way he worked, and didn't like him. Leonore might be right in saying her father always observed scrupulously any contract he signed, but attorneys were paid well to find niches unthought of.

And Ralston had no doubt that Disa hired the best lawyers he could to find those unexpected crevices in any contract.

Ralston paused at the ground floor and peered into the Quadrangle. Bacon's statue stood a lonely sentinel outside. No students. Even more to Ralston's liking, no P'torra. He slipped out into the bright, warm summer afternoon, feeling more like a sneak thief than a professor. Ralston kept to shadows and only ventured across open areas when no other path afforded itself.

He walked briskly along shady paths in the arboretum until he came to the building containing many of the University's pure research laboratories. On the second floor was one lab in particular that always frightened Ralston. But it was that room where he had to go, for only there would he find out what he needed to learn of the chaos device that had destroyed Alpha 3's civilization and caused its G5-class sun to go nova.

Ralston heaved a deep sigh and tried to calm himself. Such apprehension on his part seemed silly. Westcott wasn't a mad butcher. Westcott didn't seek his eternal damnation like the Archbishop did. Westcott didn't even care what academic sanctions Salazar might impose against him. Westcott's work was paramount, and anything else in the universe counted as trivial.

It was how Westcott pursued his researches that made Ralston so uneasy.

Ralston went up the stairs at one end of the building and hastened down the hall. At this time of afternoon, most of the researchers were in their labs. Only one or two idled in the hallway.

Ralston paused an instant before Westcott's door, then hurried in.

He screamed. He left solid floor and building to step into infinite space. Ralston tumbled and twisted in free fall, parsecs away from the nearest planet. Galaxies spiraled about in their eons-old dance and provided a ghostly light that showed how truly alone he was.

Michael Ralston fell and fell and fell.

THREE

FOR ALL ETERNITY Michael Ralston fell. He screamed but the words vanished in the hard vacuum of space, mutated and became hauntingly familiar notes that merged into oddly appealing chords and symphonies. Only slowly did he come to realize he hadn't died from internal rupturing, that the air hadn't gusted from his straining lungs, that he still lived.

Why?

"I'm a scientist," he murmured. "I will not be ruled by fear of the unknown." Easy words, and ones he accepted intellectually, but the fear still clutched his belly like a cold fist, and rational thought came only with great difficulty.

Ralston mentally retraced his path to figure out how he had come to this terrifying point. From his office, across the Quad, to the laboratory building, to Westcott's lab . . .

Westcott!

He called out the mathematician's name as if it were an ancient curse, an Earth voodoo incantation that would lift evil from him like shucking off a jacket.

"What?" came the querulous reply. "Who is it? I don't want anyone in my lab when I am . . . experimenting."

"Help me," Ralston called. Westcott's voice gave him an anchor, something to home in on. He didn't really drift aimlessly between the galaxies or hear the strange songs

25

rattling about inside his head. Whatever happened had an explanation. Ralston knew that Westcott could supply it.

As suddenly as Michael Ralston had stepped into nothingness, an ordinary laboratory appeared around him. His knees buckled and he crashed to the floor, stunned. Ralston worked his way to hands and knees and tried to quell his rising gorge. He was partially successful. The acid burning stopped just under his Adam's apple.

"Can't you read?" came Westcott's cold question. "The sign said No Admittance."

"What sign? There wasn't one on the door."

"Idiot. Fool. *Hijo de . . .*"

Ralston twisted about and sat on the cool plastic floor, back against a primitive file cabinet as he watched Westcott stalk to the lab door and fling it open. The mathematician began cursing in earnest when he didn't find the warning sign.

"Damned students think it's funny to take the sign down and then let fools like you blunder in to disturb me."

"What were you doing? I . . . I thought I was falling through space. And there was a strange song. It sounded so familiar, but I didn't really recognize it."

Ralston spoke more from nervousness than any desire to find out what the bizarre mathematician had been doing. Westcott returned to his swivel chair. His shaved head glowed in the dimly lit lab, the infrared sensor surgically implanted on the bald pate looking like some evil weapon of war. Across the room, a matching unit sat atop the computer link. Westcott had been implanted with an electrode that entered his cortex and allowed him to communicate directly with his computer.

Ralston considered few acts to be sinful or blasphemous. Allowing this surgery was one that he wished to see outlawed. It repulsed him to such an extent that he wanted to turn and run from Westcott, but the mathematician had done nothing illegal. The government regulated the implantation, permitting less than five a decade to undergo the surgery. How Westcott had qualified, Ralston couldn't say; on one wall hung a simple license authorizing the Class IV human-computer connect.

That the government regulated it and had given permission in Westcott's case, didn't lessen Ralston's revulsion.

"So slow," Westcott muttered, eyes closed. The man's face screwed into a tight bunch until his red-veined nose twitched like a weasel's. "Input is too slow. My mind can't keep up with the computer, even when I reduce the transfer rates. And it's so hard to correlate. Too many dimensions, too many tide-dependent variables."

Ralston got to his feet. The computer into which the IR sensor linked acted as a buffer for Westcott. His organic brain proved a thousand times too slow for even the slowest of University computers. A special interface computer had been built to reduce the output speed from bigger computers for Westcott's consumption. After his feeble thoughts were accumulated in a buffer, they were then squirted to the larger computer in a microburst to prevent wasting precious computing time. Ralston had heard it said that Westcott used less than a millisecond of the University computer's runtime a month, even though the mathematician remained hooked into the interface for periods up to forty hours at a stretch.

"What were you doing?" asked Ralston, calmer now. He tried not to look directly at Westcott, but little else in the man's lab commanded his attention. The single license dangling from a hook on the wall constituted the only adornment. Tables were littered with remnants of half-eaten, then forgotten meals. Westcott's desk held a standard issue console, but Ralston saw dust on the keys. What computing Westcott needed, he asked for directly through his interconnect. The far wall of the room had been outfitted with a tri-vid screen; this gave Ralston some clue as to what might have happened.

He walked to the screen and studied the touch controls. The archaeology professor shook his head. They hadn't been used in months. Dust covered them.

As quickly as he came to this conclusion, he again found himself plunging through space, hearing the tune that had haunted him before. Ralston yelped and reached out. The painful contact with the wall helped him maintain a semblance of control.

"What's going on?" he asked in a choked voice.

"Helps me think. I visualize better when I am able to surround myself with the graph." Westcott's thin frame showed eerily in the light cast by his IR sensor. "I translate data points into musical notes."

"What? Why?"

"Sounds are more transient than a purely visual display," Westcott said. "They give added dimensions when I analyze data employing time-dependent variables." Westcott smiled; Ralston thought he looked like a death's head. "I sometimes find that the sounds turn into songs that are not totally independent. It provides new ways of looking at the data. Pitch, duration, loudness, even waveshape," said Westcott, "provide new clues for me. But the waveshape—now there's an interesting factor. I can vary the pure tone of a wave down to the buzz of random fluctuations. Information falls out when I do this. So interesting. No one else at the University analyzes data this way."

Ralston made his way along the wall, found Westcott's desk and settled onto it. The feel of solid material beneath him helped hold at bay the sensation of falling forever.

"The chaos device?" Ralston asked, pulse accelerating as he understood Westcott's objectives. "You're trying to study its effects, trace its trajectory?"

"No."

Ralston's heart sank. He'd hoped that Westcott, with his unique connection with the University's computer, would be able to plot exactly the device's course through space using Alpha 3 as a point, then assuming other novas were also caused by the device's passage.

"I succeeded in that some time ago. I informed you of that."

Ralston blinked. Dotted red lines began forming in midair around him. The perspective shifted, and he floated outside the galaxy, looking inward. The curving line showed where the chaos device had been—or gone.

"I cannot ascertain direction along the line," Westcott said. "The effects of the field's passage is randomly delayed. It probably came from the far rim of the galaxy and spiraled inward in this manner." The red line vanished, only to reappear in the way Westcott suggested. A low, bone-rattling hum rose. Westcott added sound to the display to emphasize the probable trajectory. Ralston had no idea what this signified, but to the mathematician it was obviously important.

"Its point of origin is on the other side of the galaxy?"

"Some eighty thousand light years distant," said Westcott.

"We won't be exploring for the civilization that built it, then," Ralston said with some sadness. He had hoped for a *real* find—the people who had built the device. Velasquez still promised big discoveries on Proteus, and all those in the University touted him as the next departmental chairman. While Ralston cared little for such a hollow honor and added burden, he knew Velasquez had the potential for making significant strides.

That mattered far more than a chairmanship.

Michael Ralston wanted to do more than bring back alien artifacts. He wanted to find the civilization responsible for igniting the nuclear furnaces of a dozen or more stable stars and causing them to go nova. Any race with knowledge so fundamental and profound had to be worth examining minutely.

That would be the discovery of all time!

"We share much," muttered Westcott.

"What?"

"The time it would take to star to the probable planet of origin is comparable to my feeble attempts to take input directly from a block computer."

Ralston shook his head. Westcott's view of the world filtered through the computer. The mathematician saw—

and heard—everything in terms of baud rates and how inept his flesh was in accepting block circuit output. Ralston had heard it said by some mathematicians on campus that Westcott was brilliant, and this brilliance depended on his linkage to the computer. Ralston would settle for merely bright—even moronic—rather than be a slave to a machine.

Westcott might argue this point. The man might even claim it freed him to do calculations vastly beyond the comprehension of unmodified scholars. Ralston couldn't deny this, but he could deny any semblance of humanity remaining in Westcott.

"Floating in space helps you think?" he asked.

"The tri-vid display? An amusement, nothing more. As long as the computer is running, I have no trouble concentrating. The flow is like . . ." Westcott's words trailed off, then returned louder, more forceful and confident. ". . . a shining river that flows forever. I'm a leaf tossed on the singing waves. I sense so much lurking beneath the pitifully small surface I swim across, and I know it'll be closed to me for all time. But I don't mind. Not really, because most never even have the chance to ride that wondrous flow of infinite information, to get their feet wet in such incredible knowledge."

"The chaos device," pressed Ralston, not liking the fanatical light in Westcott's watery eyes. "What other information? Anything on the data I provided on possible escapes from Alpha 3?"

"Oh, that. Of course. The data proved sketchy."

Ralston's hopes sank.

"But I succeeded in pinpointing a most likely destination. Statistical confidence level ninety-five percent." On the vid screen glowed a bright orange point. "The planet is similar to Alpha 3. Only cursory survey work has been done."

"No living beings?" asked Ralston. His eagerness soared.

A preliminary survey often missed even gross planetary features. A satellite orbited a planet a few times, monitoring the usual frequencies for communications while the human scout searched geosynchronous points for satellites launched by any planet dwellers. If neither search proved positive, spectro readings were taken and a few space photos made, then the scout ship left. Space was too huge to lavish much attention on any given uninhabited planet. If for any reason a planet was needed, for research stations or even colonization, more detailed studies would be ordered as needed.

But a scout might miss a rudimentary society. The survivors from Alpha 3 might still flourish on this planet, especially if they had fallen on hard times and retreated into a more primitive culture without easily identifiable electronics.

"Call it Beta," said Westcott.

"What?" Ralston moved toward the door, upset at the way Westcott seemed to have read his thoughts. He'd wondered what they should call this system.

"Beta is appropriate, since you started with Alpha. Unless you are going to quit. Then call it Omega."

"I'm not going to quit. This Alphan named Dial left his planet without a stardrive."

"Took them almost forty years standard to arrive at Beta, then, if they succeeded in achieving eighty-seven percent light speed," said Westcott. The mathematician shrugged. "The distance between the primaries is about thirty-five light years, and I judge it difficult for a first effort to achieve velocities much in excess of 0.87c."

Ralston worked through the numbers. Forty years travel meant that almost eighty had transpired on Alpha, due to time dilation effects.

"That means they've had almost ten thousand years to colonize Beta."

"They died. High probability on that," said Westcott, almost smirking. "In that long a time, they'd have achieved planet-wide communication the scout would have intercepted. Cities large enough to see visually from space would be present, too."

Ralston sighed. Westcott was right. The more exhaus-

tive IR scans and synthetic aperture radar photos that
revealed artifacts buried under the planetary surface, were
done only if visible spectrum or ten-centimeter band communications were positive. Chances were excellent that the
refugees from Alpha 3 had died before reaching Beta, or
had perished soon after due to inimical conditions.

Their untried starship might have blown up, too. Ralston
didn't even know that Dial had reached Beta. But he could
hope that the Alphan scientist succeeded. He could hope.

As he considered the ramifications, Ralston shuddered.
They might even have carried with them the seeds of their
own destruction. It had taken ten thousand years for the
instabilities in the Alpha primary to reach nova point; the
natives had died from the effects of the chaos device much
sooner.

"It won't cost much," said Westcott.

"What are you talking about?" Ralston's uneasiness
with Westcott magnified when the man insisted on talking
in riddles. Something about communicating with the computer directly caused the mathematician to do this.

"You want to go to Beta. You need an expedition. It
won't cost much. And I want to go."

This surprised Ralston. He'd never known Westcott to
leave this laboratory. The man had to at some time, but the
IR link to the computers seemed more vital to Westcott
than any human contact. Ralston had never even heard of
Westcott having friends.

"I must gather data directly," explained the computer-
linked mathematician. "Nothing less than this will suffice
for me. The equations are so beguiling. There is an elegance
to them that doesn't exist in other systems of differential
equations. The solution to chaos will be . . . it will be
orgasmic!"

Ralston didn't argue. "When I get everything together,
you can come. Have you ever left Novo Terra before?"

"You need not worry about me. I know what to do. All
knowledge I require is locked away within the University's
computer circuitry. And it's mine, all mine!"

The IR sensor atop Westcott's shaved head began to glow more intensely, indicating harder linking to the computer. Ralston avoided breaking the beam, as Westcott had once warned him this gave the man headaches. With relief approaching release from stark terror, Ralston slipped into the corridor and shut the door to Westcott's lab behind him. The archaeologist leaned against a cool wall and took several deep, calming breaths.

"I didn't want that," he said to himself, realizing he had agreed to let Westcott accompany him when he went searching for the survivors of Alpha 3. But he had. Ralston shook his head as he went down the broad steps at the end of the hall.

He was lost in thought and didn't hear the angry voices until he exited the building. Ralston stopped and stared, then cursed his bad luck. He had walked into the center of a student demonstration. At that instant, he wished that the traditionalists had lost and the remote classing proponents had won their fight to get people off the campus and into cramped cubicles scattered about the planet.

". . . against the principles that made Novo Terra great!" bellowed a student standing on the steps of the building. Ralston didn't have to be a genius to know that they spoke about him. Many carried placards denouncing him and the menace posed by the telepathic projector. But two signs in particular hinted at the mood and composition of the crowd. "The wages of sin is death" and "Ye are fallen from grace" were scrawled with a ragged brush.

The Archbishop's displeasure with him had boiled over and taken the form of a steadily more violent crowd.

Ralston was shoved and jostled, but the students ignored him, caught up in the fiery sermon being preached by the orator. He allowed himself to bounce from one to another and diffuse like a gas molecule back to the edge of the gathering. Then he paused for a moment and saw what he'd feared—and expected.

The P'torra stood a few meters distant and worked diligently on a small device in his blubbery, stubby-fingered hand. The impulse driver recorded every word uttered, their tone and duration and the result. The small computer would return suggestions for increasing the crowd's wrath or quelling it.

Ralston had no doubt that the P'torra sought only to inflame the passions of those gathered.

The P'torra intently worked on the impulse driver and failed to see Ralston. The archaeology professor ducked behind a tall column and almost ran from the scene. The students had already been whipped into an ugly mood by the idea that Ralston had somehow committed acts against their God. The alien's gentle proddings would only push them over the edge of violence. Given such scientific meddlings, the Inquisition might appear mild in comparison. Ralston closed his eyes for a moment and pictured himself ripped apart, his parts scattered on the Quadrangle in front of Bacon's statue.

Not the end he intended. Better he die on the site of a new find, somewhere among the stars, tracking down the chaos device that had produced so much death and misery.

He knew better than to argue with the Archbishop on this point. The cleric had said that no such device could exist, that it ran counter to God's blueprint for the universe. Simply stating that it did exist put him at odds with the Church.

Ralston found one small tidbit to smile at. With luck, he could convince Chancellor Salazar that sending him on an expedition to the Beta system was better than allowing him to remain on campus. Out of sight, out of mind.

Ralston's steps turned from the narrow, rubber-paved path. He hurried toward another research building, this one untouched by a crowd's angry shouts. He wandered down the corridors until he came to an office door with three names scribbled on a piece of paper, then knocked and went in.

Nels Bernssen looked up from one of the four small desks in the room. For a moment, the astrophysicist didn't seem to recognize him. Then the man smiled.

"Dr. Ralston, good to see you. You caught me in the middle of some calculations."

Ralston knew how difficult it was to drop detailed work and cope with unexpected visitors, and the postdoctoral assistant had more than enough material to work on. Some already called the stellar instability they'd witnessed in the Alpha primary a Bernssen Condition in honor of the work done in describing it mathematically. With some additional work and a little luck, Bernssen's career would be assured.

"Sit down." Bernssen motioned vaguely toward two chairs covered with litter. Ralston didn't mind sweeping some of it off and placing it into a neat pile on the floor beside the chair. He, too, had other things to do besides housekeeping chores.

"I didn't want to disturb you but this is important," Ralston said without preamble.

"Is it about your chaos device? Leonore was telling me that you might have a good lead on its trajectory. I'd certainly like to get close enough to it for detailed examination."

"That's part of what I want to talk to you about. I think I know where refugees from Alpha 3 went."

Bernssen rocked back, his long legs curled around the chair's front legs. "For you, that'd be fine. Why come to me about it?"

"You can ask them what they saw, what they observed. A scientist—an astronomer—named Dial led a small group off Alpha 3 and toward a system we've called Beta."

"We? Who else knows about this? Leonore's father?"

Ralston shook his head. It almost pained him to admit that Westcott had done the calculations. He was heartened, though, when he saw that Bernssen's reaction to the mathematician and his mind-machine link was similar to his own.

"Brilliant, but not the sort I enjoy socially, if you track my meaning." Bernssen thought for a moment. "This Beta system was colonized by scientists who directly observed the chaos field passing by their planet? Such observations would be invaluable in determining the initial conditions in the nova.''

"We'd all benefit," said Ralston. "Westcott wants to study the mathematics of the chaos field, I want a chance to see their culture and match it with what I already know, you could get information on the chaos device. We all benefit," he repeated.

"I've got several seminars to give. Papers to write. A lifetime of work just processing the data accumulated," muttered Bernssen. "I'll be here forever." The blond smiled broadly. "When do you leave? I want to go with you. This is nothing more than dog work. I want to be where I can observe and do real science."

"I never thought of astronomy as an experimental science, but you're right." Ralston said, and frowned.

"What's the problem?" asked Bernssen. "There's something I missed. While I'm not too pleased with the idea of Leonore's father funding such an expedition—"

"He doesn't know."

Bernssen raised one eyebrow. "This is even better. Salazar has authorized your trip? I don't mind the University getting the glory, but I think IC is big enough."

"Salazar hasn't authorized it. I need your help in getting the funds."

"Blackmail, that's what this is. You don't tell me where your Beta system is unless I use my newfound leverage to get the money, transportation, and equipment."

"That's a bit blunt, and not the way I'd have phrased it."

"But it is accurate?"

Ralston nodded. The archaeology professor smiled slowly, saying, "I think Leonore might be interested in the expedition, even if her father has nothing to do with it. For her it'd be a risk having me organize the trip. But not if you did it."

"You make it sound more interesting by the second." Bernssen rocked forward and thrust out his meaty hand.

"Let's see how much the University of Ilium is willing to spend on Nels Bernssen's expedition to Beta."

Ralston shook the physicist's hand. Things were working out better than he'd hoped.

"But tell me, Dr. Ralston, if I hadn't agreed, would you have kept Beta's location a secret?"

Bernssen read the answer in Michael Ralston's cold gray eyes.

FOUR

"SO YOU AREN'T even going to say good-bye?"

The accusation came at Michael Ralston from deep shadows. His heart beat faster, and he tried to keep a quaver from his voice. He had walked through what should have been a quiet campus in a miasma of fear the past two weeks. Ralston had tried to speak with the Archbishop and been denied an audience. Seeing the P'torra quietly talking to the Archbishop's secretary a few hours later told the archaeology professor much about the reason for the prelate's rejection. He knew better than to be seen with the P'torra. The alien bore him no personal malice but would cherish the sight of Ralston being torn apart by an enraged crowd.

Ralston snorted. If anything, the P'torra was the most devoted student at the University of Ilium. He worked assiduously on perfecting his techniques using the impulse driver. By the time he graduated, he'd be expert in human manipulations.

"What do you want?" Ralston called, moving quickly to put his back to a wall.

"You've gotten paranoid in your old age." The shadow moved, changed, became a distinct figure.

"Druanna!"

"At least you recognize me." The small, sleek woman

39

moved closer and took Ralston's wrist, holding it expertly. Fingers probed until she found his pulse under the cords of muscle. "You were frightened! I'm sorry. I didn't mean to—"

"I'm all right. Things have been orbiting around me too fast lately. I thought you were—never mind. Sorry to have ignored you." Ralston was genuinely contrite. Druanna Thorkkin was a good friend, and occasionally more than just a friend. Their lives intertwined, sometimes with passion, other times with needed companionship or simple friendship. Druanna listened when he needed to talk; what he provided for her was something Ralston had never quite fathomed. Perhaps he gave her a taste of a change, a respite from their overly academic colleagues, a touch of uncertainty and wildness.

Druanna released his wrist. He didn't allow his hand to drop. Ralston reached out and lightly touched her cheek. The flesh felt warm, alive.

"I wouldn't leave without letting you know," he said. "I owe you too much."

"So you remembered, eh?" She shook her head in mock anger. "I doubt it. You're just telling me what you think I want to hear. And don't you dare stop!"

They laughed together. Ralston's arm slipped about her shoulders and he pulled her close. The comfort of her nearness turned him weak. He had been in a state of constant stress, worrying over Bernssen's expedition being grounded, not getting enough funding, a thousand details that might stop them from exploring the Beta system. Being with Druanna Thorkkin took him away from all that.

For a moment.

"How's medieval literature this term?" he asked.

"A year older, that's all. I tried out some of those authors you suggested. I'll never know where you dredged them up, but some are good. That Dupin, for instance. And Hillman. He's good."

"Hillerman," Ralston corrected. "I started reading his

work when I was an undergraduate at the University of Novo Terra. Interesting speculations on primitive migratory and farming cultures locked in those words.''

They argued over the value of the fictional work, whether a literature professor had more claim to them than did an archaeology professor. Ralston enjoyed the verbal sparring, not so much because Druanna was cleverer at it than he, but because it didn't matter. If he lost this debate, it meant nothing.

When they had wound down, the point unresolved, Ralston asked, ''How did you know I was about ready to star out?''

''Rumors,'' said Druanna. ''I guessed even more from not having seen you. What else would keep you from my bed for so long? You know I'm irresistible.''

''Not another woman,'' he said.

She turned and stared into his gray eyes as if to read truth there, then grunted and turned away. ''Damn. You're not lying. That means I'm still stuck with you.''

''You're not angling for a spot with the expedition, are you?''

''Hardly. What would a lit prof do out among the stars?''

''I'm not sure what a lit prof does here, on campus,'' he said.

''It's a good thing,'' Druanna Thorkkin said sternly, ''that you're joking.'' They walked, shoulders brushing lightly, into the deserted Quad. The last hint of summer warmth still clung tenaciously to the nighttime air, but autumn intruded with an occasional cool breeze that rippled sonorously through the leaves.

''In a way, you deserve a spot, if you wanted it,'' said Ralston. ''There wouldn't have been a sliver of a chance for me if you hadn't helped me get back to Alpha 3.''

Druanna Thorkkin had hidden Ralston while campus security had sought him just prior to his return to the doomed planet. She had even driven him to the shuttle launch site and decoyed away pursuers so that he could rendezvous in near orbit. Ralston had succeeded in getting the mental-projection equipment off planet before the primary went nova and cindered the entire Alpha solar system.

"So name something after me," Druanna said. "My idea of roughing it is not finding anything on the tri-dee that interests me. Being in primitive dig sites on dirty planets doesn't seem to me to be very . . . academic."

In spite of Druanna's athletic prowess and slim figure, he knew she was right. Try as he might, Ralston couldn't picture her out grubbing among thousand-year-old ruins and chortling over the discovery of a single pot shard or a new alloy hunk of steel. He *could* see her poring over a musty book made from ancient paper and taking detailed notes on how an author achieved a precise effect.

"Does it bother you?" she asked. They settled down under a tree, completely encased in shadow. Here and there around the Quad a yellow light shone through a window. For the most part, the University had gone to sleep.

"What? That it's Bernssen's expedition and not mine?" Ralston shook his head. "Hardly. I'm going along. It doesn't matter what they call me. Just being able to follow along the thread and maybe find more recent evidence of the Alpha civilization is important. What does bother me is not being able to fully staff my research as a result of it being Bernssen's show."

"And the chaos device?"

"That, too." He took a deep breath, held it for a few seconds, then exhaled slowly. The rush of fear he'd experienced when Druanna had startled him was gone now. "I don't think it's any menace to us. It worked past Alpha 3 too many years ago, but it's out there somewhere." He lounged back and let the soft, dew-moist grass support him. Stars burned with blue-white ferocity in the clear sky arching above.

"Chen said something about his probe being destroyed. Is there anything to it?"

"You mean any connection to the chaos device? I think

there might be. That 1054 guest star of his blew into an entire nebula. While his probes might have been destroyed by debris or any number of other things, the way they failed seems too similar to be discounted. Also, the nebula lies on the trajectory Westcott plotted for the device.''

Ralston felt Druanna shiver beside him. He couldn't decide if it came from the mention of Westcott, whom she loathed for the same reasons he did, or from the cold. Ralston decided to pretend it was the cold. He put his arm around her. Druanna snuggled close, cheeks pressing into his shoulder. Warm breath gusted into his chest.

"Seems lonely out here," Druanna said. "No one in sight. You leaving. When?''

"Just before dawn.''

"That's hours off,'' she said.

"Think we might scare anyone if we stayed here for a while longer?'' Ralston asked.

Druanna kissed him. Later, he doubted they'd scared anyone at all with their activity under the stars, and it had been the send-off he needed to assure him that returning to the University might not be such a bad thing after all.

"Does he have to go up with us?'' asked Leonore Disa. "He's already complaining.''

Michael Ralston paced back and forth, not trying to hide his nervousness. It was always this way with him before a launch. When he had been a soldier with the Nex military forces, he'd received deep hypnotic commands to calm him. That conditioning seldom worked now, unless he concentrated hard on the patterns buried in his mind. At the moment, too many people bustled about for Ralston to do that.

"Westcott is an important member of the team,'' Ralston said, not bothering to look at the distraught woman.

"You mean his funding is important,'' she snapped.

"Nels certainly did his best to get what funding he could, but we both know it wasn't enough.'' Ralston didn't try to keep the bitterness from his voice. Bernssen wasn't happy, Leonore wasn't happy, and neither was he.

Leonid Disa had done his best to block Bernssen's obtaining permission for the expedition. At first Ralston had thought it was because the man didn't want his daughter risking her life in a new and unexplored system. Leonore had coldly informed Ralston that her father couldn't care less about such things. The chairman of Interstellar Computronics worried more about Ralston finding Alpha 3 survivors who could lay significant claim to the telepathic projector. Dealing with Chancellor Salazar was one thing, buying the rights to the device from aliens with unknown ideas of money and coercion bothered him.

Even worse, Ralston guessed, was the idea that these unknown aliens might be able to construct one of the devices that the best scientific minds at the University and at IC hadn't been able to reverse engineer. Such a blow to IC and the elder Disa's ego wasn't to be borne.

"Westcott had the funds from other grants," said Ralston. "He's willing to free it for us if he can go along. Your real objection is to him, not his money."

"He . . . he gives me the heart-hops. Just looking at him makes me queasy." Leonore folded her arms under her breasts and hugged herself. Ralston looked past her to where Westcott sat.

The archaeology professor had to admit Leonore had a point. Westcott sat with an unfocused expression, his jaw slack and a tiny rivulet of spittle trickling from the corner of his mouth. The IR sensor that linked the mathematician to his precious computer lay quiescent atop his shaved head. Not until they boarded the starship would Westcott again be able to direct-link.

"What's going through his mind, do you suppose?" Leonore asked. "He hardly looks human. Makes me want to deny I'm human, and claim to be . . . to be from Alpha 3."

"They were birdlike," said Ralston. "You, my dear, are definitely and delightfully apelike." On impulse, he kissed her. Leonore stepped back in surprise, unsure of herself.

"Dr. Ralston," she said, struggling for just the right way of protesting.

"There's Nels. Let's see if there's anything more that has to be loaded before they turn on the boost laser." Ralston ignored his graduate assistant and went to speak with Nels Bernssen. Leonore trailed after, still confused.

The cold, brisk dawn wind whipping across the plains forced Ralston to pull his coat tighter around his whipcord-muscled body. Huge, silvery plumes of carbon dioxide vented from beneath the paving near the shuttle. The powerful gas laser was being readied to fire repeatedly and hurl the stubby shuttle into low orbit. Ralston avoided one of the chilling gas vents and crossed the distance to where Bernssen oversaw last minute cargo loading.

"About ready to go, Nels?" Ralston asked.

"We've got everything. I just commed the ship upstairs, and the pilot said clearance to star for Beta has come through. We'd best not wait much longer before leaving."

"You have the feeling that Salazar will rescind permission?"

Bernssen turned to Ralston and smiled slowly. "Would it matter?" he asked.

"Hell, no."

"Let's get aboard. The ground crew is starting to grumble about the weather. Let 'em squirt us aloft and get free of Novo Terra." Bernssen took Leonore's hand and together they went up the steeply sloped gangway. Ralston followed, wondering if he should alert Westcott.

Let the mathematician be stranded, he thought. They could use his grant money and not have to put up with him in space.

But Ralston saw Westcott stir, as if some unheard command awoke him. He turned like an automaton and plodded toward the portal. Ralston made way for the mathematician, who passed him without saying a word. As if he'd been in space a hundred times before, Westcott found his way to a pneumatic acceleration couch and fastened himself in with deft, efficient motions.

Ralston sprang into the couch beside the mathematician when the strident launch alarm sounded. He'd barely fastened his safety webbing when the portal hissed shut, and less than thirty seconds later the launch warning light flashed red. The laser buried under the tarmac spewed forth prodigious amounts of energy, directing the full force of its coherent beam against the shuttle's splash plate.

The heavy vessel lurched aloft, seemed to pause, then the laser recharged and again smashed into the underside. Over and over the pulsed beam blasted at the shuttle, until the whining died down signaling that they were free of most of the atmosphere. In the two-hundred-kilometer-high orbit, more than ninety-nine percent of the atmosphere had been left behind. What tenuous fingers caressed the shuttle were insignificant as it angled farther aloft to rendezvous with the starship.

Ralston closed his eyes. In less than an hour the heavy jolt told him they had docked with the starship. In another hour they had transferred their final load of cargo to the larger ship's hold and were again in acceleration couches, awaiting launch.

This time it would be for a star system so distant the Beta primary wasn't even visible from Novo Terra.

"The pilot's not very communicative," observed Bernssen. "He shut off the screen showing the cockpit."

"There aren't many who socialize with their passengers," said Ralston. "They claim it keeps them from peak efficiency."

"Verd, but I like to watch the controls," said Bernssen. "Not that I could do anything, but I want to know if anything goes wrong."

Ralston turned and looked at Leonore, who shook her head. Ralston said nothing. If Bernssen's worst fears came true and something happened to the pilot, Ralston knew that Leonore could operate the complex computers that drove the starship. She might not be a licensed pilot, but she know enough to get them back to a planet. He wondered why Leonore hadn't told Bernssen about this particular skill of hers. Would it have annoyed the physicist?

"We're ready. He's got us lined up for the shift," she said. Her body tensed, then relaxed beneath its webbing.

It took no pilot to know that they were on their way. The starship gave a deep-throated rumble as the shift engines powered up. Rockets flared and pressed them gently into their couches. Before Ralston could even call out "good luck," the pilot ordered the shift.

Blackness grabbed at Michael Ralston, pushed him into the couch, shut off nose and mouth, hammered at his chest, then pulled him inside out before showing him all the colors of the spectrum. Every shift affected him differently, and this one combined pain with beauty.

But through it all, he exulted. The Beta system and answers lay ahead!

Ralston tucked his knees to his chest, performed a quick rotation, and straightened just in time to grab an elastic band to stop himself. He had adjusted to the free fall quickly, and spent the nineteen weeks starring to the Beta system going over all the material he and Leonore Disa had accumulated on Alpha 3. In addition, Bernssen had shared the information he had garnered from the Alpha primary's spectral analysis before it had gone nova.

Only Westcott had remained aloof and uncommunicative, floating in a cocoon of silence, the pale red light in his sensor flickering on and off as he presented problem after problem for the small on-board computer to solve.

"We know so little about this field causing the random behavior," said the astrophysicist in a voice loud enough to be heard by both Ralston and Leonore in the low pressure chamber. "At least the pilot starred us within a day's travel of the most likely planet."

"Beta 5," mused Leonore. "It looks so like Alpha 3. They might be twins."

"Dial might have known it would be similar," said

Ralston, "but I think he just guessed. The Alphans didn't seem adequately advanced to have sent out survey probes that could return with the information needed for colonization."

"What courage," the woman said. "To set off with a sublight drive, perhaps not even knowing what you'd find at the end."

"With the chaos wracking the populace on Alpha 3, did they have a choice?" asked Ralston. He remembered all too clearly the devastating problems the residual effects of chaos had caused. One of his graduate students had died from an epileptic seizure induced by the field, and several of Bernssen's fellow researchers had been similarly affected. The chaos effect distorted electrical transmission, turned chemical reactions into chance rather than energy-gradient-driven occurrences—and it had triggered instabilities in the star that, ten thousand years after passage, had caused it to explode.

"They had no choice," Ralston stated firmly, now sure of himself. "I know them as well as anyone since I've been through so many of their dioramas. The telepathic lessons might not have been perfect for me since I'm not of their race, but I learned enough to know that they had no choice."

"Still," murmured Leonore. "Such a long trip, possibly generations, depending on their speed."

"Westcott said it might have taken up to eighty years planet time for them to arrive here," said Bernssen. "I think his estimate is close for a sublight velocity starship."

"It's a pretty planet, but there's no EM emanations," said Ralston. "I checked my own equipment."

"We'll get a few satellites in orbit," said Bernssen. "Then we'll know for certain."

"Be sure to send out the radar-imaging satellite in the first launch," said Ralston. He heaved a deep sigh. "I expect we'll have to sift through ruins once more."

"Just because they didn't send a greeting party doesn't mean the planet's devoid of life," said Leonore. "They might be cautious. After all, for them it's only been about ten thousand years since all the trouble on Alpha 3.''

Ralston laughed without humor. He floated to the center of the chamber, legs slightly bent and arms loose at his sides, the most comfortable position in free fall. By distancing himself from the others, he floated into an eerie silence. The lowered air pressure made it more difficult for sound transmission and, as long as he stayed away from the metal struts supporting the boron-fiber composite walls, he got no vibration from the ship's massive shift engines. He might as well have been cast into that awesomely infinite well he'd experienced on blundering into Westcott's lab.

Leonore and Bernssen began going down their checklist. Much of the work had been done using automated equipment; this had allowed them to bring fewer human personnel and the requisite support material. Still, Bernssen had ten assistants—and Ralston had to rely on his own two hands and Leonore's. He needed Bernssen's ten scientists and a hundred more besides, but he knew better than to complain.

He was here! He had left behind the University and again starred to where real science could be done.

Bernssen gave the signal that he'd popped out the first of his recon satellites, then sent Ralston's synthetic-aperture radar satellite into polar orbit around the planet. Ralston stiffened a few minutes later when Bernssen's control panel blossomed red. The archaeology professor scissorskicked and he got himself moving slowly, until he snared a line and pulled himself to where Bernssen and Leonore worked feverishly.

"What's wrong?"

"My probe's glitched on me. Signal turned thready, then winked out."

"What about mine?" Ralston demanded.

Bernssen shook his head. "Looks fine, so far. I missed the calculated orbit a bit. A bit too much eccentricity, and the other orbital parameter's wrong. Call it a hundred kilometers too high, but that's within equipment limits."

"The second probe is ready, Nels," said Leonore.

The astrophysicist launched it. As with his first satellite, this one also sent back a continuous data feed that turned to inexplicable white noise before dying.

"I checked those myself. Zero defects on both. On all my equipment. Hell, what else was there for me to do for over three months while we were in stardrive?" Bernssen looked guiltily at Leonore, as if she might contradict him. But Ralston's graduate student was as absorbed over the loss as her lover.

"Try a third?" suggested Ralston.

"Not yet. We'll let yours relay back its data. That might give some idea what's happening. We're still a few hours from orbit ourselves. We might not want to stay."

"A radiation belt? Micrometeorites?"

Nels Bernssen looked at the archaeologist, a curious expression on his face. "There might be more," said Bernssen. "The residual effects of the chaos device on Alpha 3 might be stronger here. They might have brought it with them."

"Your calculations are inadequate, sloppy, and lacking in the necessary rigor," Westcott said, and all three jerked around. "I have analyzed the fleeing aliens' course to this system."

"So?" asked Ralston.

The mathematician smirked, and said, "The poor bastards failed to run away from the path of the chaos field. They followed it backward, possibly by accident or ignorance, but they ended up in this system."

"What are you saying, Westcott?"

"The chaos field had already passed through the Beta system twenty-three hundred years prior to their arrival. The Alphans didn't run away from it, they ran *into* it."

Michael Ralston's eyes turned to the probe control panel. A new red light winked on. His probe had just died of equipment failure, too. Chaos held Beta 5 firmly in its sway. There was no chance at all now that he would find any survivors of the Alpha system. None.

FIVE

"Definitely instability in weather patterns," said Michael Ralston, straining to move a crate containing excavation equipment. He blinked as heavy droplets pelted down into his face. He wiped the rain off and levered the crate to a spot where he could open it under a slanting plastic roof set up for this purpose.

They had grounded four days earlier, after a week in orbit. None of their probes had failed after the first three; retrieving those satellites had shown what Ralston had feared, however. The block circuits had simply ceased functioning. The only explanation for the massive solid state failure had to lie with the residual randomizing effects of the chaos device.

Ralston had repaired his radar-imaging probe and done a quick survey of Beta 5, finding only two widely separated sites likely to produce any results archaeologically. Of any survivors from Alpha 3 he found no trace at all.

The laborobots had toiled ceaselessly since grounding and produced a tiny village of plastic huts. Some were set aside as living quarters, but Bernssen had used the largest to set up his stellar-probe equipment. A few satellites orbited the planet, and from those the astrophysicist took constant readings.

"Michael, the ultrasonic digger's finally ready," said

51

Leonore Disa. "I've got the supervisor hooked into it. All
we need to do is program the path, and the equipment will
do the rest."

Ralston wiped more rain from his face, turned and
perched on the side of the crate. He didn't like the prospect of letting the sophisticated guidance system do work
he enjoyed. There was no personal thrill in having the
ultrasonic diggers operating day and night. He *liked* grubbing about, eyes alert for any hint of a discovery. He *liked*
the feel of dirt sifting through his fingers as he worked out
the complex history of the society whose ruins he researched. But Ralston would be the first to admit that they
were shorthanded and that the complex supervisor computer was more than adequate for the task of monitoring
excavation. If anything of note appeared in the digger's
maw, an alarm would sound and let him do what he liked
doing.

Ralston snorted in disgust. He had to admit that the
supervisor and the robots connected to it would do a
better, more efficient job than the group of graduate students he'd had with him on Alpha 3. The machines wouldn't
blunder about and destroy precious information through
ignorance or carelessness or simply not caring.

That had been the point that troubled him the most.

The students—except for Leonore Disa—simply hadn't
cared. Two had been rehabs—criminals whose brains had
been chemically and electrically altered to the point of
destroying any initiative or curiosity. The others had merely
put in their time, hoping to complete the equation Physical
Presence = Advanced Degree.

All except Yago de la Cruz. That student had been
hungry for notoriety and honor in his family's eyes. It had
robbed him of both caution and his life.

Ralston shuddered at the way de la Cruz had died. The
student had been seized in an epileptic fit induced by the
Alpha 3 telepathic projectors. The chaos-caused epidemic
had ravaged the alien society near the end of their civiliza-

tion, and somehow this seed of madness had been implanted in de la Cruz and cost him his life.

Ralston looked out over the gently rolling, verdant hills of Beta 5. A lovely world and one not as obviously being destroyed by the chaotic conditions inflicted on it by the passing device. Trees rose to admirable heights not ten kilometers away and formed a forest Ralston vowed to explore. The flora and fauna of this world seemed harmless enough. His eyes dropped to the neat lines marked out by the digger, the first of the ruins being revealed. Whatever had killed off the last of the Alpha 3 refugees, it wasn't inimical wildlife.

"Pretty, isn't it?" said Leonore.

She sat beside him on the crate. The rain had cooled the day considerably, but the woman wore only a halter top and shorts. A bright silver plate and injector connection just above her navel marked her medport. Ralston knew she used various recreational drugs and direct-injected them through the med-port, but an old-fashioned stubbornness clung to much of his own actions. He didn't like the idea of anything running through his bloodstream that didn't belong there. Out in the field it made life easier if he didn't "need" chemical recreation.

He knew most of the current faddish drugs favored by the students were non-addicting. On occasion he might partake himself. But having a medport installed in his belly struck him as a modification that went against all logic and good taste.

"Verd," Ralston agreed, looking across a tiny stream of crystal clear water. "It's hard to believe that the chaos device passed by this planet."

"The weather makes it easier to believe," said Leonore. "It's just as bad as on Alpha 3. Unpredictable. I've had the computer trying to formulate an accurate weather forecast for three days. No good. Random results over any period longer than a few minutes, even though the planet's only got a twenty-degree axial tilt that should moderate the climate."

"Maybe that's the way it should be. Don't you get a little bored with the weather on Novo Terra?"

"No. Why should I?"

"You know what it'll be at any given time. There's no surprise, no thrill of a sudden rainstorm or unexpected sunshine when you've braced yourself for clouds."

"Some surprises I can live without." Leonore peered out from under the plastic roof. The sun shone brightly, a few fleecy white clouds drifting through the azure sky before the faint outlines of both moons clung. Only minutes before it had been raining.

"The digger's started," said Ralston. The ultrasonic hum filled the warm afternoon air. The supervisor recorded every grain of dirt in its block circuits for future analysis. "We ought to get the other two running, also. Cuts down on the time before we find something."

"This was the only other ruin on the radar?"

"This was it," said Ralston. "That bothers me. If Dial reached Beta 5 and they had any success colonizing, there ought to have been more cities."

"You've verified the other ruin?" asked Leonore.

Ralston frowned. "Verd, and it's on the other side of the planet, almost antipodal to this ruin. That strikes me as odd, unless the refugees had a falling out. After forty years aboard their ship, maybe they couldn't stand each other and decided to split their forces. Otherwise, I'd think their best chance for survival would be to stay in as large a group as possible."

"The evidence from their culture shows how revolted they were by epileptics," said Leonore. "Perhaps they isolated those showing the symptoms of being touched by the chaos field."

"We'll find out soon enough."

Ralston looked up to see Nels Bernssen walking through the muddy area in front of the equipment shelter. He waved to them and came over.

"The poor stupid bastards," the physicist said.

"What are you talking about, Nels?" asked Leonore.

"The Alphans. They left their home to get away from the destruction going on in their society, and where did they come? Here. Beta 5 had already seen a pass-by from the chaos field."

"Westcott's sure of that?"

"It's definite." Something in the man's tone alerted Ralston.

"What do you mean?"

"I just finished a preliminary data analysis," said Bernssen. "This is going to make me damned famous, and I don't much like it."

"Nels, no!" Leonore's stricken cry matched the cold knot forming in Ralston's belly.

Bernssen nodded grimly. "The so-called Bernssen Condition is present in the Beta primary, too." He laughed without any humor. "Life is hell when you find yourself getting famous off something that will destroy any future research."

"How long do we have before the sun goes nova?" asked Ralston, seeing a repetition of his disaster on Alpha 3.

"Hard to get quantitative about it. There's nothing pressing. But we've definitely got a run of bad luck on it. I'd say within a planetary year."

Ralston had hoped for more. The rough estimates placed a Beta 5 year at a half standard year. From the planet, the G8 primary seemed only half as bright as normal, giving the impression of perpetual descending twilight.

How appropriate, he thought. Darkness always falling. The slightly heavier gravity wore on him almost as much as this new and unwanted information. He didn't ask Nels if he was certain. Ralston had enough confidence in the astrophysicist to know that the data had been analyzed properly. The 5600-degree Kelvin temperature of the sun's surface would begin to rise, hotter and hotter, cool slightly, then rise uncontrollably and beyond belief until the star exploded.

Perhaps a planetary year—six months—until this occurred, Nels had said. Ralston thanked the planet's slower rotation and thirty-three hour days. If he had little time to work, he could at least work most of it in the dim daylight.

This gave him enough time to poke about in the ruins, but probably not enough to completely exhaust all available data. Still, he wouldn't be under the pressure he'd experienced on Alpha 3.

"Looks like another storm moving up fast," said Leonore, pointing to the horizon. Clouds lead gray with moisture accumulated and rose in a terrifyingly immense thunderhead. Strong upper winds sheared the top into a familiar anvil pattern. Already tiny sparks of lightning formed to light the dark underbelly.

"There's not much the rain will harm." Ralston looked over the ruins where the digger had uncovered a neat masonry wall. "If anything, it might wash off the dirt and help us out."

The words were hardly out of his mouth when the ground began to quiver. Ralston felt as if he'd been on an all-night binge and his knees had turned to putty. He wobbled and grabbed for support, thinking perversely that the fault lay within him rather than outside. A stroke? Did he suffer momentary dizziness from working too hard?

"Quake!" bellowed Bernssen. "Get out from under the shelters and into the open. Where's that hijo Westcott?"

Ralston went limp and let the motion of the moving surface toss him about. He hit and rolled and tried vainly to stand. The best he succeeded in accomplishing was to balance himself on hands and knees. The world spun around him, and his gut felt as if it had turned to jelly.

"It's a bad one, the worst I've ever been through," called out Bernssen. The physicist had one arm around Leonore, but she pushed him away, preferring to weather the violent natural assault apart. Ralston watched the couple bounce together, then rebound and fall to the suddenly treacherous ground. They bobbed up and down before vanishing from his line of sight.

Ralston held back his nausea and a sense of helpless-

ness. The quake seemed to go on forever. He looked about
and saw crates being overturned by invisible hands, the
supervisor blinking wildly that its mechanical minions had
ceased operation, the plastic shelters tumbling down from
unexpected stresses.

Then the rains hit with a fury that Ralston hadn't believed possible. It wasn't enough that the planet rattled his
teeth. Now the skies had to open and drench him.

"Quake's about over," he heard Bernssen calling from
some spot on the other side of their compound. "Reading
has it at 5.9 Richter. Wasn't all that bad. Just a light
temblor."

Ralston doubted this. The shaking had been severe enough
to throw him off his feet. But when he peered through the
curtain of rain all around, he saw minimal damage. The
supervisor had restarted the ultrasonic diggers, and the
parts of the shelters that had fallen wouldn't take more
than a few minutes to snap back together.

The archaeology professor checked the instruments, satisfied himself that none of the programming had been
altered by the quake, then went to see how Bernssen and
Leonore fared. They grumbled at the rain but gamely
worked to get the roof lifted back onto a shelter. Ralston
walked on briskly to find Westcott.

"You in there?" he called out. Westcott's shelters had
sustained minor damage. "Are you all right, Westcott?"

No answer. Ralston tugged open the sprung door and
moved it to one side. Within the shelter he saw no light.
The heavy clouds had cut off the feeble sunlight, but
Westcott hadn't set his interior for automatic illumination.
Or if he had, the quake had damaged the control circuits.

"Westcott?"

A pale red light winked balefully: Westcott's head-
mounted sensor. Ralston entered the room and knelt beside
the mathematician, taking a pulse. The beat of the man's
heart proved strong. Ralston took Westcott by the shoulders and turned him so that he stretched out supine. As he
did so, one accusing eye opened and speared him.

"What do you want? Interrupting me is not something I appreciate, especially when I am in the middle of such intricate and demanding calculations."

"Sorry," Ralston said without meaning it.

"Worst of all is breaking my direct-link beam with the computer. I told you that gives me a headache." Westcott fought to sit upright. He appeared weak.

"We had a quake. In case you didn't notice, it brought down most of the buildings in the compound. I worried that you might have been injured."

"You were worried about me?" asked Westcott, as if this were more complex a statement than even the most esoteric of the higher geometries he studied. "I was working out the mathematics governing your culture's death."

"The Alphans?" Ralston wondered at the mathematician. How could he have not noticed the world shaking all around him?

"Yes, yes, of course. Who else?" Westcott pushed past Ralston and stepped into the rain. He immediately returned, hands covering his sensor. "A hard failure in the planet's geologic structure," he said unexpectedly.

"The quake?"

"A product of topological dynamics. I must add that to my set of equations. You see," Westcott said, as if Ralston really cared, "there are two types of failure: hard and soft. The soft failures occur with some regularity. Small strokes in humans, minor memory lapse, that sort of thing. No real importance. The hard failures constitute the epilepsy you've found."

"You're saying the planet just had an epileptic fit?"

"Don't be ridiculous," scoffed Westcott. He seated himself in front of his computer console and made minute adjustments to the IR sensor pickup on it. Satisfied that his link had been fine-tuned, he went on. "Nonetheless, it is a hard failure, a solution only slightly different for the set of nonlinear differential equations governing crustal plate movement." Westcott's IR sensor blinked on and off slowly— the man "thought."

"Can you predict if there'll be more quakes? We might want to move to a safer area."

"You don't understand, do you? The model for weather is a complex set of equations in which even the smallest disturbance will cause chaotic behavior. A falling leaf will trigger instability. How can you avoid such minor movement?"

"I didn't mean the weather. I meant the . . ." Ralston swallowed hard when he realized that to Westcott weather and quakes were simply different manifestations of the same equation set. *Any* movement might trigger a new quake since the passage of the chaos device had forced randomness on the system.

"The time evolution of any system obeys strictly deterministic laws," said Westcott, "but your chaos field has caused the system to act as if it obeyed only its own free will." He chuckled. "I am sure the Archbishop would be tempted to say this is God's will at work, but it can't be. It is random. Enforced randomness."

"I've got to check my equipment for damage," Ralston said, wanting to be away from Westcott. The mathematician took away what little hope he had.

Ralston left, hardly noticing the rain hammering away at his face. He squinted and walked through the mud and murk to the excavation site. The quiet humming of the digger reassured him that not all in the universe fell prey to chaotic dynamics.

He dropped to his knees and looked at the debris produced by the digger, knowing he wouldn't find anything of consequence but wanting to make sure that neither the supervisor nor digger hadn't glitched for a moment during the quake and missed something. The archaeologist found only bits of rock and insignificant organic matter that had been caught in the digger's maw.

"Michael," came the faint cry. He looked up. The rain obscured his vision farther than a few meters. Again came the plaintive call. "I need you."

"Leonore?" Ralston stood, trying to decide the direc-

tion of the woman's voice. But it hadn't sounded like
Leonore. Not exactly. He swallowed hard. It had sounded
more like Druanna Thorkkin. He pushed such an absurd
notion away, but uneasiness grew like some evil seed
within him. "Druanna?" he called.

"Here, Michael. Here!"

He turned slowly, unable to pinpoint the source of the
voice. He bent down and wiped off the casing atop the
ultrasonic digger. Using his thumbnail, he pried back a lid
to expose the programming console. He poked a few times
until he hit the proper buttons.

"Michael? Come to me. Now!"

The digger let out a beep and slowly turned until it faced
outward, in the direction of the copse he had noted earlier.
Rain hid the trees—and whoever called to him. Ralston
reprogrammed the digger to return to its mindless chewing
away at the dirt around the ruins.

He set his inertial tracker to be sure he wouldn't get lost
in the downpour, then started out across the grassy plains.
Ralston knew it wasn't Leonore Disa who called. And he
couldn't quite decide why he didn't return to find her and
Bernssen to tell them what he'd just heard. It wasn't pride,
or fear that they might laugh at him. Ralston had been
scorned and ridiculed by the best and lived through it.
Curiosity moved him—but what else?

He swallowed, tried to get enough spittle to spit, and
failed. The voice sounded so much like Druanna, yes, but
even more like Marta. There had never been another woman
in his life like the vivacious Marta, now lost to him. It
couldn't be her, not on Beta 5. But who was it?

What was it?

"Michael, hurry. Please!"

His pace across the meadow remained constant even
though he wanted to break into a headlong run to discover
who played such a cruel joke on him. Bernssen? The man
seemed affable enough, but did he wrongly suspect anything between professor and student? Ralston felt only
admiration for Leonore Disa—and nothing more intimate.

She had aided him when he needed it, and he'd seen that she received all the accolades due her for their discoveries.

But what if Nels Bernssen was jealous? Would he take the opportunity to kill the archaeology professor?

Ralston considered this ridiculous, but the voice did draw him.

He slipped once in the mud and stayed on one knee, listening intently. The rain slackened, but the weather continued its onslaught with fiercer winds. Cold and wet, he now had to fight against winds he guessed to be gusting to at least sixty kilometers an hour. Ralston shielded his eyes with his hand. The sun cast strange shadows through the clouds and rain, turning the landscape into something surreal.

Ralston checked his inertial tracker and found the green arrow pointing back to camp. He almost spun and followed it to safety. But the voice sang out again and drew him. He remembered one of Druanna's stories, an Earth folktale about creatures living on rocks along a river. Their voices called out and hypnotized sailors, drawing them and their vessels to the rocks where they wrecked and died.

"Michael! I need you!"

Ralston moved on, not bothering to wipe off the mud on his pants leg. He walked with a springy step, the heavier gravity of this world unnoticed now that he walked toward . . . who? He felt stronger and confident in his ability to handle anything. What could be in the small forest? Their sensors hadn't picked up any large animals.

He skirted the edge of the forest, moving to put the pale orange sun at his back. If he discovered something eager for dinner, Ralston wanted the feeble rays of sunlight slanting in under the storm clouds to work for him, not against him. Even a momentary blinding would allow him to escape, he was sure.

"Who's there?" he called out.

"It's been so long, Michael," came the hidden voice. Closer, Ralston noted a peculiar twang unlike either Marta

or Druanna. Definitely female but not . . . quite . . .
human. Too much bass undertone.

Leaves rustled. Ralston moved to put a tree trunk at his
back. He peered in the direction of the noise. A flash of
intuition told him that this was a ruse. He dropped to one
knee just as a heavily taloned paw circled the tree and
ripped away bark. That might have been his face if he'd
reacted a nanosecond slower.

"Madre de Dios," he gasped, moving away. Ralston
fumbled for the call button on his tracker. Once activated,
Leonore would be able to home in on him. She might even
come immediately.

Or she might not notice for hours, if she and Nels were
together or if she worked to put the compound back in
order after the quake.

"Michael," the creature called. "Come to me." It
lumbered around the tree and gave Ralston a clear look at
it. Almost as tall as the archaeologist, the beast was stock-
ier, possessing muscles that rippled like an ocean's waves
under a scraggly brown fur coat. Its mouth opened to
reveal double rows of teeth. But it shut its mouth, and he
again heard his name called.

Ralston feinted to the left and dived to the right. The
creature followed him with contemptuous ease. He barely
missed having an arm clawed off for his effort. Ralston
grunted and kicked away, blood trickling from four narrow
gashes in his shoulder.

"Michael, come closer."

The long snout opened, and heavily muscled jaws clacked
shut. Ralston saw that it'd be impossible for this creature
to speak in a human voice. He postponed any further
speculation on the source of the voice when the creature
dropped to all fours and rushed him. Ralston rolled away,
picked up a fallen limb, and used it as a clumsy club to
hold back the creature. The beast rolled itself into a ball,
then exploded with claws lashing out. Ralston received
another set of scratches on his right leg. More painful than
dangerous, the wound bled freely.

Ralston cursed his hubris in not bringing a weapon. Then he laughed. What weapon would he have lugged with him? This was a physics-archaeology expedition. They hadn't brought any weapons with them. Mass had counted aboard the starship. Superfluous equipment had been left on Novo Terra. Never had Ralston heard of an expedition where a member had been attacked by indigenous wildlife.

It was his bad luck to be the first. All he had to do was live to write it into his research paper.

"Stay back," he shouted, hoping the sound of his voice would frighten the creature. If anything, it emboldened his attacker. Ralston managed to find another dried limb, this one devoid of smaller branches. He swung it like a bat and connected squarely with the beast's snout just as it opened its mouth.

Ralston felt teeth breaking. Claws raked just centimeters away from his stomach. He danced away, swinging his weapon.

"Michael, why is this?"

He swung again, putting all his strength into the blow. It crashed hard on the beast's sloping shoulder. Ralston couldn't kill it, but he hoped to drive it off. If it broke off its attack for just a few seconds, he could run. Even in the heavier gravity—with fear to lend speed to his retreat—he thought he could outdistance this predator.

The creature circled to put itself between him and the camp.

"Michael, I am hurt. You shouldn't do this to me."

Ralston blinked. He straightened and looked at Marta.

"I've changed," she said. "Please help me, Michael. You hurt me. Help me now."

"I—" he began.

Sharp talons tore with impossible speed at his vulnerable left side and drove him to the ground. The slender woman's body turned back into the heavy creature. It reared up over him, ready to make the death stroke across his throat.

SIX

"WHERE'S MICHAEL?" ASKED Leonore Disa. "I want to ask him about starting on a new area in the site. The ruins just to the north look more interesting from these photos than the one we're working on now."

Nels Bernssen didn't look up from his work as he shook his head and said, "Haven't seen him recently. He went to talk with Westcott after the quake. He might still be there."

"I just looked. Westcott's sitting in the corner of his shelter all glassy-eyed and thinking his computer thoughts."

"I don't like him, either," Bernssen said, finishing the adjustment, then straightening to pull Leonore into the circle of his arms, "but he's useful. Before we're finished with Beta 5, you'll see. We might have to use him as a paperweight, but he'll be useful."

"Michael said that Westcott is responsible for the calculations leading us here. That still doesn't make me like him any more. He . . . he's hardly human."

"You're the one who deals with alien cultures."

"I'm only a grave robber," Leonore joked. "I do awful things with their skeletons."

"Want to do wonderful things with mine?" asked the astrophysicist.

"Depends on what you had in mind." Leonore kissed

him. The sound of rain gently falling outside the plastic
shelter soothed her. The quake had come unexpectedly,
and she needed Nels' assurance that everything would be
all right. She received it.

The talons flashed downward in an arc, catching the
orange rays of the setting sun and turning them into bloody
spikes. Michael Ralston's combat experience saved him;
the Nex had hypno-trained him well to respond to attack.
He jerked to one side, then exploded past the deadly
talons. He slammed hard into the bole of a tree, re-
bounded, and pulled himself to a sitting position. He
kicked out at the creature and drove a foot into the back
leg, finding the knee joint.

The beast dropped forward on all fours, giving Ralston a
chance to get to his feet. He wobbled, and blood seeped
from the wounds he had already received, but fear had
been purged from him by the hypnotic commands. Cold,
clear thought showed him the precise location on the creature's neck.

Ralston swung the tree limb club, and the impact of
wood against flesh rocked him. Weakness assailed him—
but the beast broke off its attack. Whining, it lumbered
into the depths of the forest.

Ralston almost collapsed as the adrenaline flow subsided. He fell to his knees, breathing hard.

"Marta," he said softly, looking after the creature. But
the archaeology professor knew that he hadn't really seen
the woman he'd loved so long ago. Her image, her voice,
had been projected into his mind. He now saw how he had
supplied the details that had been missing. The voice
wasn't quite right, but it had been close enough. The
image wasn't perfect, but it had taken him aback.

Those were all the creature had intended—or needed. It
was a predator laying a complex trap.

Ralston held onto the tree trunk for support. What had
gone wrong with their survey? No large animals had been
detected. Another equipment failure? Or had he just been

in too big a hurry to get started on the excavation and ignored the evidence?

He hated to admit it but there hadn't been time to do a complete workup of the data collected from orbit. The IR scans might have shown a creature that size if he'd made the effort to find it. Carelessness had almost cost him his life.

"But what a fabulous creature," he said softly. "How did it come to learn to hunt like that?"

Ralston checked his wristcom. The alarm button had been depressed. He peered out in the fine mist and looked for Leonore or Nels or any of the others to come to his aid. No one. Nels' researchers wouldn't be monitoring his com frequency, he decided; Leonore and Nels were the only two he could reasonably expect to respond.

He heaved himself out into the open, following the green arrow that pointed the way back to the compound. As he walked, he felt better. The thicker air supplied needed oxygen to his laboring lungs, and strength returned after the initial surge of fear. Ralston held a bit of torn shirt over his shoulder wounds; the compress stanched the bleeding and helped the blood clot. By the time the plastic shelters came into view through the drizzle, he felt almost human.

He made his way to the shelter set up with the automedic. The small, mobile robot hummed and whistled to itself as Ralston sat on the floor in front of it. Tiny metal probes worked across the surface of the wound, checking for deeper and more serious injury. Finding none, the automed gently held the edges of the cleansed wound together and sprayed plastiskin over it.

"Thanks," Ralston said when the automed had finished the last of the scratches. "Take a blood sample to make certain the chemistry is normal. I don't want to pick up any strange infections." He winced as the automedic obeyed. Ten millimeters of blood came from a vein and another five from an artery for blood gas analysis.

Ralston pulled away and rubbed the two punctures. At

repairing humans, the robot was unparalleled, but it lacked much in the way of bedside manner. Ralston always vowed to check the automed's programming to make certain it hadn't been given a slight vindictiveness in drawing the blood.

A beep sounded. Ralston glanced at the readout on the main console. He heaved a sigh of relief. As far as the sophisticated mobile unit could tell, he hadn't been invaded by any alien microbes.

"Michael, what happened?" came Leonore's worried voice. "We were passing by and heard the automed's signal." She went to the console and studied the data still displayed. "What did this to you?"

"That's a good question," said Ralston. "I've been thinking about it while the robot worked on me—I'm all right. Don't worry about that." He quickly told of the attack, then said, "This might seem far-fetched, but we've never found any other creature that hunts telepathically. More to the point, it recognized me as prey."

"You're saying this might be an animal brought to the planet by the Alphans?"

"Could be," said Ralston. "Or it might be a native creature who learned to live off the Alphans. They looked a great deal like us—humanoid, bilaterally symmetrical, about the same height and build, if you ignore the details of our features."

"It might have been waiting a long time between meals," said Bernssen. "If the refugees died off very long ago—and it looks as if they did—what's this creature been living on?"

"That thought occurred to me, also. It seems possible that it isn't naturally a telepathic hunter. What if it blundered into one of the Alphans' dioramas and learned about them—and even became telepathic itself?"

"You may have hit your head. Did you have the automed check for concussion?" scoffed Leonore.

"The chaos device passed by this planet much longer ago. That had to affect the native wildlife in some way we can't even begin to guess at. What if the creature blundered into a diorama and the combined effects of chaos and the projection turned it telepathic?''

"A mutation?" asked Bernssen.

"More like an adaptation. Call it a mental scarring. It might not be able to breed true—most mutations don't. But it might have made its nest in a diorama. Over the years, it not only learned that Alphans were acceptable food, but also how to project the images. It didn't find Alphans but it did find us—me."

Leonore and Nels exchanged glances. "All right, all right," said Ralston. "I haven't the slightest idea what's happened with the beast. Maybe every creature on this world is telepathic."

"Not likely," said Leonore. "The other creatures wouldn't fall prey to such mentally projected images. They'd adapt or learn to tell the difference." She cocked her head to one side and asked, "What image did it lure you with? You didn't say."

Ralston ignored her, not wanting to dredge up memories best left untouched. He said, "Let's look for the creature and track it to its lair. I think we'll find another Alphan diorama."

"Let's track it down, no matter what we're likely to find," said Nels. "This beast is dangerous to us all. What if it sent out a mental attack while we slept? It might lure us from camp one by one, and we'd never know until it was too late."

"We don't have anything to kill it with," said Leonore. "No weapons."

"Fix up a spear," said Ralston. "I'll put a small battery pack on it. If we can't stab it, we can shock it."

"I'll have Melendez or one of the others start on a perimeter alarm, too," said Bernssen. "I want to know what comes and goes through the camp."

Leonore glanced at Ralston, saw that her professor was well tended to by the robot, then hurried after Nels. Ralston sat on a hard chair and considered other explanations for the telepathic beast's presence. No matter how he twisted logic, he kept returning to a combination of chaos— Westcott's topological dynamics—and the Alphan refugees' thought projector.

He rose and left the shelter, the sun setting just over the horizon. The gusty winds had blown away the clouds, and once more the sky shone clear, clean, and perfect.

"I don't like this," said Leonore Disa. She looked apprehensive about stalking through the darkened woods hunting the beast that had attacked her professor. "What if it's a nocturnal animal? It'll be able to see us better than we can see it, even with the IR glasses."

Nels Bernssen tugged at the night goggles, trying to bring them into adjustment. He failed.

"I was out at twilight," said Ralston, checking the meter on the device he held. "That means it's crepuscular. We have the chance to track it down now, while it's gone to its burrow."

"It might live in the trees," said Leonore, glancing into the shadowy, leafy masses above them. "Arboreal."

"The limbs were wrong for that," said Ralston. "There. Got it. I've locked on to its trail."

"What is that thing?" Leonore asked irritably. She glanced around, visions of huge monsters leaping at her. "I hope it's better than your spear."

Ralston smiled. The spear had been a jury-rigged nightmare. The best they had been able to do was file down the sides of a piece of scrap steel and mount it at the end of a long plastic tube. Running down the inside of the tube were the wires Ralston had attached to the steel knife. By thumbing a contact at the far end, a sizable electrical jolt could be produced. He had no idea if it would kill the beast, or even stun it, but he knew it would produce some effect. And if it didn't, the spear itself would serve well.

Ralston had to grin at the thought of venturing out like savages with a primitive spear. All the tri-vid dramas had the mighty interstellar hunters equipped with power rifles capable of leveling cities and sonic devices that stunned through the sheer power of their pulsed shock waves. He thought they were carrying weapons more in line with the way it should be done. The more primitive you went out, the better chance you had of returning.

He didn't want to be any creature's dinner, and this kept his senses at their peak. Ralston knew that both Leonore and Nels were similarly on edge. They might jump at the slightest unusual sound, but they reacted rather than letting it pass by.

"This might not work in a city, but it's performing well out here where there's nothing to confuse it," he said, indicating the tracking device Leonore had mentioned. "The surface acoustic wave caused by its scent is picked up by a transducer. The internal block circuit then gives me a readout on the meter. Anything less than twenty-percent deflection is a lost signal. About eighty percent is strong."

"You're really able to track its scent using a sniffer?" Leonore shook her head in wonder. "I've used the damned things to scout out poison fumes in underground dig sites, but I never thought of using it like a bloodhound."

Ralston laughed. "You'd be surprised at some of the ways I've used sniffers. With the right block circuit inside, you can differentiate between male and female phero-mones and . . ." Ralston's voice trailed off. He didn't want to get into what he'd done while a graduate student at the University of Novo Terra.

"I don't see any hint of heat trail," said Bernssen, pulling off the bulky IR-powered goggles. He held them out to Leonore. "You want to use them?" The physicist wiped his forehead clear of the accumulated sweat and dust that had dammed up above the goggles' headband. Leonore shook her head.

They trooped through the forest, Ralston maintaining a sixty-percent deflection on the meter. Gradually, the reading mounted until it hit an optimal level. Ralston stopped and slowly turned to take in the entire area. Only in one direction did he pick up a strong reading indicating the beast's passage.

"There," he said, pointing toward a dark spot in the forest. He took the IR lenses from Bernssen and handed the sniffer to Leonore. The terrain jumped about until his eyes adjusted to the ghostly imaging created by the sensors. A heat vent glowed brightly in the night. Clutching the spear, Ralston advanced one slow step at a time until he stood at the mouth of the crevice leading down into the ground. A large boulder protected one side, and a fallen, rotting log the other. The creature had found itself a well-protected home.

"Different readings from below," said Leonore, frowning. "There's the creature, but I'm picking up something else. Looks familiar, but I can't place it." Ralston heard her fiddling with the sniffer.

"Well?" he asked. "Decided where you've seen similar readings?"

"No, except . . ."

"Except on Alpha 3," he finished for her. "In the dioramas."

"The Alphans?"

"Our beast might prove itself an ally. It just might have found a burrow in the very spot we've been looking for so hard." Ralston adjusted the ungainly goggles to a more comfortable position, then dropped to hands and knees and stuck his head into the crevice. "It'll be a tight squeeze, but I can make it."

"You're not going in there!" protested Leonore.

"She's right," spoke up Bernssen. "You need more than that pathetic spear if you're going to crawl into a monster's lap."

"It wasn't that much of a monster. Dangerous, verd, I'll agree with you there. It's strong and quick, but it thought it was safe hunting with the telepathic imaging. Finding its lair here explains how it came by its only real talent."

"So the creature did get it from the dioramas," mused Leonore, fascinated in spite of her uneasiness. "It sounded far-fetched before, but it looks as if you were right, Michael. The combination of the chaos device's residual effects and the Alphans' projector allowed it to develop usable telepathic talents."

"We've got one way of finding out for certain. Any of those back in camp biologists?"

"No, just astrophysicists," said Bernssen. "My department—and Westcott's—did fund this expedition, after all." He sounded apologetic.

"We can always put it on ice." Ralston trembled a little when he mentally finished, As I did with de la Cruz's body. He shook off the troubling thought. "I'll leave my wristcom on to record everything. Track me with the sniffer. All my scent parameters are in its block memory."

"Michael," said Leonore, touching his shoulder.

"Verd, I'll not take any foolish risks." He heaved a deep, calming breath. "At least no more after this one." With that, the archaeology professor slid forward into the darkness.

Through the infrared lenses the tunnel took on a surreal, red, shimmering aspect. Ralston ignored this and pushed forward, keeping the tip of his makeshift electric-powered spear in front of him. If the creature had chosen that instant to attack, Ralston would have been helpless. He couldn't thrust well while wiggling on his belly, and he couldn't reach the contact that would send the charge into the electrified steel tip.

Ralston found the passageway dirty and littered with odd bits of debris—and no trace of the creature that had attacked him earlier in the woods.

"Whew," he said, as heavy animal musk assailed his nostrils. If he'd kept the surface acoustic wave detector, it would have overloaded. Ralston tumbled out onto a floor unnaturally smooth beneath the detritus. He held back a sneeze and carefully studied his surroundings. For the benefit of his wrist recorder, he said, "I've entered a long, artificial corridor. The walls are bare—no, there are murals painted on them. Visual spectrum light is required for clearer reading. It appears to me as splotches of light and dark, with only a slight difference between pigmented and bare wall.''

Ralston walked slowly, glad that he could stand upright. The stench almost overwhelmed him when he rounded a right angle and came into the creature's lair.

He turned slowly and studied the larger, open area. No sound reached his ears. The odors were too overpowering for him to pinpoint the beast's whereabouts. And the IR goggles revealed no living heat source. What they did reveal, though, sent Ralston stumbling forward, oblivious to any danger that might be in hiding.

"Dioramas! I've found them!'' He took a few deep breaths, regretted it when he choked, then forced himself to breathe in shallow pants. He reached out with the tip of his spear and traced over the faint outlines of the statues inside the first diorama. Carefully, trying to keep his voice level and at a slow, clear pace, he described all that was visible.

Ralston became enthralled by the little he could see— and how he wanted to enter those dioramas and learn the telepathic lessons he knew awaited there!

"I am staying in the central area,'' he said with more than a little sadness, "because of the lack of light. It was found on Alpha 3 that a general idea of the subject of each diorama could be formed on the basis of composition, number of characters and their relative positioning within the scene.''

Ralston continued to dictate as he wandered, oblivious now to the odors around him. Once he flipped off the IR goggles and found himself plunged into total darkness except for the brief More's secondary lightning flashing within his eyes. Ralston turned on the power once more to the IR goggles, relieved at the ghostly images that reappeared. The irrational fear always struck him that he'd become permanently blind when he experienced such darkness. It had never happened, but intellectually knowing his sight would still be there and emotionally knowing it proved two different things.

Ralston made a careful circuit of the large area from which all the dioramas appeared to radiate, then stopped at the end farthest from the hallway where he had entered. A circular hot spot showed at about waist level.

He probed gently with his long spear. The resulting heat surge in his goggles, and the force with which the spear was batted from his hand, took him by surprise. He'd unexpectedly found where the creature had holed up.

The beast exploded from the circular opening. The slight delay between the IR goggles sensing the heat and the small block circuit actually showing the image on the lenses worked against Ralston. He saw, but always a fraction of a second too late.

He grunted and stumbled in the detritus on the floor. Feet slipping from under him, Ralston fell heavily. Above, he saw the beast rearing. The slight pause before it made its attack saved him. He instantly jerked and rolled to one side. A talon raked his back, but the creature's death stroke had missed its target. Ralston kept rolling and came to hands and knees, gagging as he sucked in huge lungfuls of the fetid air.

He spun and kicked when he saw the heat-shimmered bulk come for him. The animal may prefer hunting at twilight, Ralston thought, but its night vision was incredibly acute. Or did it track him with another sense? Had it learned to stalk by its prey's thoughts?

His foot connected with a hairy leg, and the creature yelped in pain. Ralston had done it no significant damage, but he had forced it to break off its attack.

For a few seconds.

He took in a deep breath to shout for help. Bernssen and Leonore were less than a hundred meters away. The tiny crevice and corridors would funnel his cry.

Ralston gasped as the creature ran full tilt into him. One sloping, powerfully muscled shoulder drove into his midriff. He felt his diaphragm crushing under the impact and could do nothing about it. He smashed into a wall. Feeble kicks at the predator did little more than enrage it.

The archaeology professor spun to one side, sustaining deep gashes on his flank. He groaned at the pain. He couldn't outfight the beast. He had to retreat.

Ralston forced himself upright and looked around. The shining red blob had to be the creature. A rectangular glow in the other direction was the entry point. Ralston stumbled, righted himself, then ran as hard as he could for the opening. If he reached it, he might be able to slither back up to the forest.

Even as he ran, he discarded that idea. The beast was more agile—and it was the creature's tunnel. It hadn't dug a way in and out that would be hard for itself.

Ralston changed his plans as he reached the corridor. He'd yell. Bernssen and Leonore would come and help him. The creature wouldn't want to fight off three humans. It'd retreat. It'd go back into its small hidey hole.

A powerful blow to the back of his head sent Ralston sprawling. Stunned, he turned onto his side. All that the archaeology professor saw was the towering red heat outline of the beast. It prepared for the death stroke.

SEVEN

THE INFRARED GOGGLES tilted on Michael Ralston's head, giving him a skewed picture of the creature—but there could be no doubt that death was an instant away.

Ralston shrieked and tried to kick at the beast. His legs refused to obey. He'd fallen and gotten them twisted under him. His head rang like the University carillon. The outcry did nothing to stay the attacking beast. It reared and, for the first time, Ralston heard it growl deep in its throat.

It knew victory lay only a quick stroke away.

At the beast took a step forward to make the death slash, it grunted and slid to one side. Stepping on the shaft of the spear it had batted from Ralston's hands, the beast had stumbled. The brief pause in the attack allowed Ralston to drag himself a few centimeters farther away.

The enraged animal struck out at the spear—and gave Ralston his first real chance. The spear bounced from the animal's claws, rattled into the wall and fell at Ralston's side. The archaeology professor picked it up, touched the contact at the base, felt the electric surge along the shaft, then braced himself.

The creature snarled, rose and threw itself on him. A vivid electric spark blinded Ralston as the creature touched the electrified steel tip. Then the plastic shaft began warp-

ing as the weight of the creature bore down. Ralston
fought to gain his feet but dared not let loose of the spear.

It was all that kept death at bay.

Talons dripping with his blood slashed just millimeters
from his face. Ralston felt their passage as fetid air gusted
into his nostrils. He turned and twisted and worked the
spear deeper from the creature's heaving chest. The battery
continued to send galvanizing jolts into a primitive nervous
system. By the time Ralston pulled the spear free, then
thrust hard at the dim form outlined in the IR lenses, he
knew the animal was more dead than alive.

He finished the chore with three more weak stabs.

Gasping, Ralston reeled away, spear clutched in hand.
He reached out to brace himself against a wall but missed.
He yelped in surprise, then fell heavily into the first diorama.

Ralston tried to escape the scene before the telepathic
projector began its message. He was too weak; as he
straightened, the familiar tingling sensation at the fringes
of his mind began. Rather than struggle, he resigned himself to ride out the lesson programmed into this alien
diorama.

"Dial, we can't do it!" came Querno's sobbing words.
The tall, thin avian being held hands over his face to hide
his shame. Ralston-Dial's sympathy went out to his friend.
They had been through so much. And now they failed!

"No," said Ralston-Dial. "There is still hope. All our
world is in flame. Valiant comrades die in disgrace before
our eyes—" Ralston-Dial shuddered at the mere thought
of such dishonor as the epileptic fits brought to both victim
and observer—"but we will succeed. They laugh at my
theories, but I *know* we can do it." Ralston-Dial stroked
Querno's close-feathered scalp ridge.

Ralston-Dial gasped. The scene changed from a burned-
out hut to the oil-tang-scented hold of a large, clumsy
spaceship. A curious otherness assailed him. He knew this
ship lacked stardrive capacity. It looked wrong. But at the
same time, it looked right. It had been *his* dream brought
to fruition.

"We launch soon, Dial?" came the fledgling starship captain's timorous question. Captain Fennalt fussed about the cockpit, long, thin fingers stroking the controls as if they might come alive under his ministrations.

"There are others escaping the city," Dial said. "It isn't seemly hurrying away when our journey will take so long."

Fennalt nodded, stretched his long arms, then settled into the acceleration couch contoured to fit his body. He curled his feet around the perch bar and tried to relax. "You are sure of this star? It will take us away from all misery?"

Dial bobbed his head up and down several times in agreement, but he said nothing. He feared he might betray his uncertainty. This star showed a spectral pattern of bands and dark and bright lines similar to their sun. No astronomer had ventured a theory, at least in his hearing, about the chance of finding another planet, much less a planet capable of sustaining avian life circling a distant star.

But Dial saw no other possibility. They had to take the desperate gamble. If a pitiful few might flee the planet and escape the carnage and madness seizing the populace, their race might continue to thrive. Honor demanded that they try. Dial's curiosity also drove him, but mostly honor dictated his course.

This similar star lay the closest to home—and its distance was incomprehensible to him. His skills were in engineering, not in the wild imaginings of star travel. Hadn't the Council of Rules decreed that no space travel, even within the confines of the solar system, be attempted? It had been for the best, Dial knew. The comet that had so stirred the interest of an entire world had also betrayed them.

The dark comet had passed within a few planetary diameters but had produced no coma, no tail, no evidence of the spectacular gases boldly predicted by scientists and expected by the populace. This had been two hundred years before, but Dial had seen the disappointing pictures. Space travel had been dealt a death blow.

Dial prayed for those who had already died. In his mind, the connection between the dark comet and those slow, dishonorable deaths was firm. The dark wanderer through their system had sprayed poison gases into their atmosphere and doomed so many.

It must have. No other explanation came to him.

Dial kept his breathing shallow and slow, his chest barely moving. Through this he would escape, as had the others going with him on this desperate trip.

"It is difficult to believe," said Captain Fennalt, "that the first real expedition from our planet will be one of such tremendous duration and daring."

Dial silently signaled for Fennalt to begin preparation for the rocket blast. He tiredly went to quiet those already in their couches, especially Querno.

Ralston-Dial felt the acceleration. With the crushing pressure on his chest came a curious exaltation. The first star voyagers! They were rocketing for the stars!

Ralston coughed, stumbled, and braced himself against the wall of the diorama. The lesson had ended. Sweat beaded his forehead, and his side had turned stiff from his oozing wounds and the caked blood. Ralston kept one hand on the slick surface as he guided himself from the scene. To have done anything else might have proven dangerous for him. He knew each of the figures in the diorama carried a distinct telepathic lesson told from their individual point of view.

He could see the lift-off from Alpha 3 through the eyes of both Fennalt and Querno if he wanted.

All Michael Ralston wanted at the moment was to rest, to sleep, to sleep for a million years. Cold, tired, weak, he used the warped spear as a crutch.

And this betrayed him. He planted the butt end of the spear on a slippery patch. The support he relied on so heavily squirted from under him. He fell headlong, his heavy IR goggles flying from his head. As the archaeology professor stood, he realized he had gone farther than he'd intended.

Another projector beam touched his mind and imprinted its eons-old message.

". . . Dial," said Querno, "this place is as dangerous as our Far Home."

Ralston-Dial looked at his friend. How could an intelligent person such as Querno not realize the awful truth?

"Querno," Ralston-Dial said, heart heavy with what he must say, "you do not understand. This planet was clean before we came to it. It is *our* presence that tainted a virgin world. We've carried the diabolical gases with us."

"The trip was costly," admitted Querno. Scores of the refugees had died during the long, long sublight speed journey. Fennalt had pushed the ship to ever higher speeds, but the barrier of light speed eluded them, as Dial had worried that it might. Barely had they reached ninety-percent light speed. But the void of interstellar space provided them with the molecular hydrogen fuel needed for their scoop. They had accelerated for twenty years.

Ralston-Dial knew that they had been in space for almost eighty years, even though, for Dial and Fennalt and Querno and the others fleeing Alpha 3, it had seemed little more than half that.

For the Alphans, this concept of time dilation lay far in their physical and mathematical future—a future they would be denied because of the chaos device.

"Costly, yes," Dial went on, "and we carried the seed of destruction with us. We planted it on this world."

Ralston shook all over, wanting to call out to the avian scientist, to tell him how wrong he was, how the chaos device had already passed through the Beta system and left its swath of wrongness. The telepathic projector strengthened its hold on him; Ralston was forced even more into the scene, assumed Dial's persona even more.

"We've tried all the ancient purification rites. They failed," said Querno.

"This is not a matter of spiritual belief," said Dial,

exhausted from his research. "I have failed to detect the gas. I wonder if the others might not have been right. Perhaps it was an electromagnetic field that has somehow infected us." Dial shook his head, tears welling up to run down his hard nose.

"Our two cities are distant enough so that one might survive if the other perishes," Querno said. "Fennalt leads the other well. He finds new rooms daily."

"Has he discovered who built that city?" asked Dial.

"No. But the buildings are useful. Fennalt will flourish. He is a proud and honorable man."

Dial shook himself all over and made mock-preening gestures, a remnant of times long past. "It will do no good dividing our forces. We have journeyed so far and so long only to die. Look around, Querno. Can't you see this is so?"

Querno squawked and protested. "We fight, Dial. We will not surrender to these alien influences."

"Yes, yes, we fight. But it is in vain. Look and you see only men and women of honor disgracing themselves in increasing numbers. They flop and thrash about and there is nothing we can do to bring them back to their senses. Just as before, just as it did on Far Home, this curse works on us in the most degrading way possible."

Dial looked from the roof of the one-story building. The world appeared so invitingly gentle. But he knew the raw fury the capricious weather brought with it. One day they enjoyed peaceful summer, the next brought ice storms. As soon as the arctic weather turned, they might experience autumn or summer—all at random. The true miracle lay in how the world's wildlife coped with such virulent change.

But it did, as they did. Life refused to give up even a tenuous grasp. Dial saw that as both a blessing and a curse.

"We've got to get him out," exclaimed Nels Bernssen. "We can't leave him locked up in there. Look! He's bleeding. That damned animal clawed him badly."

"No, Nels." Leonore Disa held the physicist back. "We've never pulled him from one of the dioramas before it had run its full message. I'm not sure what might happen to him if we tried it now."

"He's bleeding to death! There's no telling what internal damage there might be. *Madre de Dios*, Leonore!"

"Nels, please." The woman held him back. "If you go into the diorama, you'll be caught up in it, too, and be no good to Michael. It's a risk leaving him there, but less a physical one than the mental ruin we risk pulling him out."

"*Hijo de puta,*" Bernssen grumbled, caught on the horns of the dilemma. "What possessed him to go into one of those damnable scenes in his condition?"

Leonore had no answer. The evidence on that point was less than clear. Ralston had killed the beast with the spear, then mysteriously gone into the diorama on the left. The sniffer showed definite and lingering human body pheromones there. Leonore adjusted the quartz light they'd brought.

Ralston had crossed the floor, then entered the diorama directly across from the first one. The professor now stood within, locked with the peculiar muscle rigidity characteristic of the telepathic projector's operation.

Leonore wanted to take the chance, to drag him out before the lesson had run its course. But she stood and watched and waited. Better to turn Ralston over to the automedic for a long stay than to do damage to his brain.

"How long do they usually run?" asked Bernssen.

"We know so little about them. I suspect that these aren't designed to run long. They are museum exhibits—at least, the ones on Alpha 3 were."

"So the crowd wanders in, gets a short lecture, then moves on?"

"Something like that. But these might be different. These might be—probably are—left to tell the history of their travel and all that happened to them once they landed on Beta 5."

"You're saying he might die of starvation before the field releases him?"

"I doubt that," said Leonore. "After all, the Alphans were physically similar to us. They must have eaten on a regular basis. They wouldn't want to kill themselves by going for days or weeks inside a diorama. Nothing indicates their mental makeup was too divergent, either. That means their attention span wouldn't exceed a human's by much. He . . . he should be out of the scene soon."

She hoped that were true. Ralston had been locked within this one for at least an hour. It had been that long since she and Nels had ventured down the crevice after returning to the camp and getting the portable light. They had blundered into the room and found the creature dead of stab wounds—and Ralston already within the diorama.

"The one next to him. He shows up in all the scenes," said Nels. "He must be the leader."

Leonore had to agree. And Ralston had assumed a pose next to the leader, which probably meant that he had to endure the longest lesson of any within the diorama.

Leonore wandered around the small chamber, impatiently waiting for something to happen. She was peering at the scene next to Ralston's when Bernssen yelled, "He's coming out. I saw his eyes blink. And look. His color's changing."

"He's turning white. What's wrong?" Leonore took a step forward but Bernssen held her back. She stopped, her hand on his. If she'd entered as she'd impulsively tried, she might be caught up alongside Ralston. They both might be trapped and helpless.

Her professor stumbled out and dropped to his knees just outside the diorama. He looked up with haunted gray eyes. His lips moved as if he tried to speak.

Then the epileptic fit seized him.

EIGHT

MICHAEL RALSTON'S ENTIRE body stiffened, then he began snaking about on the floor with a series of uncontrollable convulsions. For him the world turned into a white glare; for those watching, it became a nightmare of helplessness.

"Don't let him bite his tongue," cried Leonore Disa. She tried to hold the thrashing Ralston and failed. Even the much stronger Nels Bernssen had difficulty. By the time the large physicist had gotten his knees onto Ralston's shoulders in a schoolboy pin, and Leonore held the man's legs, the worst had passed.

Ralston blinked and opened his eyes, not seeing.

"Are you all right?" Bernssen asked nervously. One hand went to Ralston's forehead and came away sweaty. The archaeology professor's eyes focused now.

"Can't breathe too well with you sitting on me like that. And something seems wrong with my legs. Can't move them at all. It's dark, too."

Leonore and Bernssen slowly released their grips. Ralston stirred weakly. If he had been mauled repeatedly by the creature whose lair they'd invaded, he couldn't have felt much worse. The claw marks throbbed, but it was the rest of his body that suffered even more. Every joint, every muscle, everything refused to function—except to send out a signal of dull, aching pain.

85

Bernssen helped him sit up. "Why did you go into the diorama? The dioramas," he amended, the proof of Ralston going from one to the other visible on the floor from the disturbed debris.

"Didn't mean to," Ralston said. His throat barely worked; he knew how the ancient criminals felt during a hanging. He spat, took a few deep breaths, and decided against trying to stand yet. "The resident of this fine suite of rooms didn't take kindly to me invading its lair. It came for me, I killed it, then staggered back. It was an accident that I fell into that scene." He pointed to the one showing Dial, Querno, and Captain Fennalt preparing for takeoff.

"Then you came stumbling out and fell into this one?" asked Leonore, hardly believing such an incredible story.

"I wouldn't have dared it," said Ralston. "Not in my condition." He squinted into the quartz lamp. "How long has it been? For me it seems like about fifteen years."

"A little longer than an hour. We were afraid to come crashing in on you, so I went back to the compound and got the lamp while Nels stood guard. When I got back we decided to come down to see what had happened to you."

"Wish you'd come sooner. I could have used the help." Ralston's gray eyes darted to the fallen animal. He regretted having to kill it. With some luck, they might decide how the creature had come to hunt by sending out its telepathic bait. If nothing else, the xenobiologists at the University would have gotten a thousand publishable research papers from studying it.

"You scared us when you came reeling out of the diorama," said Bernssen. "That fit looked just like the ones that took my researchers back on Alpha 3."

Ralston frowned. "I had a fit? I don't remember—wait! I *do* remember. But I didn't have it. The seizure was Dial's. He—" Ralston stopped, trying to sort out the confusing array of facts, half memories, and telepathically infused knowledge.

He went pale when he figured out what had happened. "The convulsions *are* projected," he said. "We're going to have to be extremely careful examining the later scenes. After de la Cruz's death, I suspected it, but this is certain.''

"Salazar would shut down their project to duplicate the machine if he knew," said Leonore with some glee. "And Daddy will be horrified. He's so conscious of IC's reputation. Any hint that mental disorders can be projected will kill all their research."

"That's be the wrong thing to do," said Bernssen. "We need the knowledge. If anything, such a projection technique might help psychologists correct their patients' problems."

Ralston said nothing. He knew how the telepathic projector would be used. With crime a constant and increasing problem, the government psychologists would first try it as a new method for criminal rehabilitation. Rather than burn out their victim's brain with chemicals and electricity, they'd use the Alphan projector to impress the new, "normal" behavior patterns.

Ralston had just seen firsthand how effective it might become. He shook himself. To dwell on such negative aspects of a new technology hid what good might actually come from it.

Still . . . to be rehabbed that way was a new form of mind death. And what of the newsers? They always sought fresh ways of enhancing their news-report ratings. A trivid screen coupled with such a projector might prove the unraveling of society. No matter what the newser said, the audience would believe it absolutely.

"This is dangerous," he said. "We've got to try to learn how it works." He made a gargantuan effort and heaved himself to his feet. "If for no other reason, we need to protect our minds from it. The Alphans had the same problems, I'm sure. We're supposed to be archaeologists. We can find out how they really used the dioramas."

Ralston looked around the chamber in wonder. The refugees had crossed, for them, infinite light years of space to flee the effects of the chaos device. They had only

run into the jaws of the chaos, landing on a planet already
in the throes of ruin.

"Let's get out of here. I need some repair work done."
Ralston touched his injured side and winced, a wave of
nausea breaking over him. "And I want to make notes of
all I've discovered. There's something I can't quite remember that seems significant. But it's hard for me to
concentrate."

He slumped forward. Leonore caught him as he fell face
forward, unconscious. She and Bernssen dragged Ralston
through the small tunnel leading to the forest. A full-blown
winter storm pelted them with sleet all the way back to the
compound.

"How's excavation coming?" Ralston asked.

"That's not the usual question," said Leonore Disa.
"You're supposed to ask, 'Where am I?' or even 'How
did I get here?' "

"I know where I am," Ralston said. The plastic walls
and the partially emptied equipment crates told him that
much. They had brought him back to his shelter. The other
question seemed equally amenable to logic, even in his
weakened condition. Leonore and Nels had been responsible for returning him to camp. His side had been expertly
mended: the automed's work. The only thing bothering
him was the chilly air. He commented on it.

"We're in the midst of a heavy winter storm," said
Leonore. "It hit while we were in the creature's lair."

"But it was autumn. Or spring." Ralston experienced a
moment's dizziness. Parts of his memory had become
blocked. The seizure had a greater adverse effect than he
cared to admit.

"Westcott says it's a product of the chaos field. His
dynamical variables are all being altered, sometimes on a
second to second basis. That's why we're getting winter
now."

"Snow?"

Leonore nodded.

Ralston sank back onto his cot and silently cursed. "The diggers aren't having any problem, are they? I've found it hard keeping them going when the temperature dips down too low. Something about moisture and their block circuits. The manufacturer denies it, but they start going off course, sometimes by as much as a radian per hour. When I worked the Transients' site on Icefloe 6, I had to chase one that had decided to run off. Got it just before it tumbled off a cliff into a lake of freezing water."

"The supervisor is taking care of all the corrections. It's a good machine." Leonore chuckled. "After all, it's made by IC."

Ralston's mind spun and whirred as it struggled to put into order all the things he needed to say.

"Westcott. Get him. I've got some information he might be able to use."

"Getting him away from his computer is hard. His IR link doesn't work outside his shelter. In rain or snow it's even harder for him to keep an interference-free link. Absorption on the transmission frequency, he says."

"Can Nels rig him up a relay?"

"Verd, but IR absorption in a snowstorm will still make it a futile project."

"Dammit, I *need* to talk to Westcott." Ralston forced himself to sit up. The world oscillated in crazy arcs.

"Don't, Michael. Please. I'll see if I can appeal to Westcott's sense of decency." She snorted derisively. "And when that fails, I'll grab him by his implanted sensor and drag the hijo over here. Is that verd with you?"

"Do it." Ralston sank back, his thoughts already on what he had discovered in the dioramas.

In less than ten minutes a wet, cold, and angry mathematician blundered into the shelter. Westcott sat down, crossed his arms and glowered at Ralston.

"Good to see you, too, Westcott," Ralston said. The sarcasm failed to penetrate Westcott's ire at being separated from his precious computer. Ralston fleetingly wondered if Westcott had ever considered a portable unit. The idea died as quickly as it had been born. Such a unit would be too feeble for the mathematician, he decided. Nothing but supercomputer power appealed to the direct-linked researcher.

"Work on this for me," said Ralston, the snap of command in his voice. Westcott sat straighter, ready to protest. The coldness in Ralston's gray eyes silenced any such outburst. "When in the second diorama, I experienced a seizure—or rather, the character whose identity I'd assumed did. This projected convulsion must be prevented if we're to continue. How do we prevent the seizures from happening?"

Westcott shrugged. "Drugs. Chaotic dynamics seems an appropriate method for calculating which ones, what dosages, their effective durations. It seems little more to me than a parameter resetting. A boundary condition here and there . . ." Westcott shrugged.

"What do you mean?"

"Any reliable mathematician should be able to calculate how to prevent the chaotic bifurcation. See," said Westcott, beginning to warm to his lecture, "a tiny change in just one parameter throws the entire system into random behavior."

"The leaf falling causes the tornado," said Ralston, remembering that part of Westcott's theory.

"Verd, this abrupt change in the system characteristics comes in response to a single parameter alteration. Normal behavior in humans must change to chaotic as a result of neurons and neural networks shifting due to the telepathic projection."

"To prevent bifurcation, some dosage of a drug will suffice?"

"That seems plausible to me." Westcott closed his eyes. His lips moved silently. He finally gave a half smile. "Yes, it is plausible. What drug, I cannot say. You'd need a medical doctor to advise you, but this procedure is possible."

"And?" Ralston prodded.

"The implications go beyond preventing these mal seizures." Westcott hugged himself and rocked back and forth as he spoke, his eyes lit by an inner fever now. "Heartbeat irregularity. That's a product of chaotic behavior. Bifurcation occurs and fibrillation destroys the normal rhythms. And there must be some cellular mechanism that—"

"Causes cancer," Ralston finished for him.

"Why, yes, yes!"

Ralston licked dried lips and burrowed down into his cot. Dial had never admitted it—his culture denied any public show of physical weakness—but there had been the subtle fears of cancer. A word crept upward, one he only barely understood, "Neuroblastoma."

"That seems a distinct probability," said Westcott. "Coupled with the neural and network instability, cancers of the nervous system would be the most likely to be transmitted by your telepathic projector. The oncogene might be triggered." Westcott sat back, pleased with himself. Ralston had to admit that, even without the direct-link to a computer, Westcott seemed a formidable intellect.

"The Alphans might have been dying of cancer as well as the more obvious epileptic effects," he said. "And it can be transmitted through the dioramas?"

"High probability," agreed Westcott. His eyes focused on the wall and he muttered something. "The equations governing all this . . . what degree of reproducibility can I obtain in the calculations? A tricky set of pseudolinked nonlinear differential equations."

"Work on calculating the dosage to prevent the convulsions," ordered Ralston. "Hook your computer directly into the automedic. Use its pharmacy library."

"Yes, good, very good." Westcott rose and walked from the shelter, not bothering to close the door behind him. A steady blast of wintry air threatened to freeze Ralston. He staggered to the door just as Leonore returned.

"I'll get it," she said.

Ralston pulled the thin insulating blanket around him. It

trapped all his body heat and should have made him unbearably hot by now; he was still cold.

"You get what you needed out of . . . him?"

"Westcott's peculiar," agreed Ralston to his graduate assistant's unspoken appraisal, "but he might be the one who lets us explore with impunity." He quickly outlined Westcott's search for the precise equations governing the bifurcation.

"We use the automed, then go in? That's all?"

"I hope so. If we'd brought along a more powerful automedic, I'd be happier about trying it."

"You need your rest. I'll go into the next diorama." Ralston started to deny her permission, then stopped. She was a researcher, just as he was. Leonore knew the dangers and, as much as he hated to admit it, she was the better choice. She had a med-port imbedded in her stomach. With a supervisor hooked into a network with the automedic and Westcott's computer, Leonore's condition could be monitored continuously and any needed drug administered swiftly. Even more to the point, Ralston knew he wasn't able to withstand another session in one of the scenes. Not soon, at any rate. He healed rapidly, but the automed hadn't been able to manufacture much synthetic blood to replace what he'd lost. The small field unit was intended to be used as a first-aid robot, not as a full-fledged hospital doctorobot.

"I can do it, can't I?" Leonore asked.

"I want full recording. If Nels can be there, I want him. And I'll be there, too, even if I can't participate directly." Ralston thought on it. "I wonder if the scene varies if two people enter. Would Nels be willing to try?"

"You must have hit your head," Leonore said, brown eyes wide in surprise. "Where's the stuffy old prof who won't let anyone take a risk, except himself?"

She sobered when she read his expression. "You think it's that serious a problem?"

"More than the chaos device causing normally stable

stars to explode. More than the entire race of Alpha 3 perishing. More than weather disturbances.''

"You're trying to tell me we've got to solve the question of where the chaos field came from?''

"More. We've got to track it and stop it. Look at the . . . well, the chaos it's created. And while talking with Westcott, the idea came up that it might trigger oncogenes.''

"We'll get cancer?'' Leonore shrugged. "Unfortunate, but that's hardly much of a problem. Not with our medical technology. If a gene toggles on, we can toggle it off.''

"The types of cancer the chaos field might cause are swift acting. We might be dead before we even detected it.''

"I'll order weekly automed tests. Or should we do it daily?'' Leonore cocked her head to one side and listened. The mournful howl of the winter wind had died. She opened the shelter door to syrupy warm sunshine. "Daily,'' she said with conviction.

Ralston drifted back to a fitful sleep, dreams of oncogenes and bifurcation and randomly changing seasons troubling him.

"The digger froze,'' said Nels Bernssen. "I tore it apart and looked at the guts. The heavy rains had soaked in around its seals, then the cold snap froze the water. Part of a block circuit cracked. The rest of the damage is minor.''

"Can you reprogram?'' asked Ralston.

"Hard to make the time to read out the old circuit and burn a new one,'' the physicist said. "My own research is reaching a critical stage. We finally got enough satellites up and working to do a good study of the primary. Solar activity is increasing, just as it did back in the Alpha system.''

"Any immediate danger?''

The tall blond smiled. "Are you asking if the Bernssen Condition has been achieved yet? The answer's no. The Beta sun won't go nova for some time yet. My new best estimate is a minimum of a standard year—two planetary years. We've got time to study it.''

"It's hard for Leonore and me to keep up the excavations by ourselves,'' Ralston said. He looked out over the partially cleared field where the ultrasonic digger had been working. About a quarter of the structural foundations poked up nakedly above the muddy, half-frozen ground. "We've got to make plans for exploiting the dioramas, too. Full spectrum photos, surface acoustic wave, a dozen other things. The information gleaned there might be more important than learning how the refugees lived here.''

"You're trying to say that because I have a staff of researchers with me, and you've only got Leonore, that I ought to help you?'' Nels made a wry expression. "Get Westcott into the field. He's pasty-faced. The air will do him good.''

"I know your work's important,'' said Ralston, "but we're unlocking the effects of the chaos field on people. The avians were similar enough to humans to put them in a parallel taxonomic branch.''

"Xenobiologists would dispute that.''

"Let them,'' said Ralston. "An entire world was destroyed due to the effect of that chaos device. I'm wondering if it wasn't a weapon that got out of hand.''

"It wasn't the product of the Alphans,'' said Bernssen. "That much is apparent.''

"All the more reason to study the problems and learn to cope with them—and then find the chaos device and stop it.''

"Go starring off in some random direction to hunt for a comet-sized gadget that'll scramble our circuits and brains? You archaeology researchers aim high.''

"What if the chaos field passed by Novo Terra? What if there're several orbiting around the galaxy? What if it's a natural phenomenon that might spring up anywhere at any time?''

"Work on studying the induced solar nonperiodic behavior is as important,'' said Bernssen.

Before Ralston could shift the argument in an attempt to persuade Bernssen to devote more time to the archaeological side of the expedition, a heartrending shriek tore the crisp, cold air.

"What in the name of the Trinity was that?" demanded Bernssen. He craned around, seeking the source of the piteous outcry. "It wasn't human."

Ralston went into the equipment shelter and worked for a few minutes on the supervisor. He had programmed in a signal response to everyone wearing a wristcom. All those in the field sent back satisfactory responses.

"No one's in trouble," Ralston said. "It must be another animal."

"We haven't seen any since you killed that mind-baiting creature."

"That worries me, too," said Ralston. "How can a solitary creature survive? The biome requires a certain population for species propagation—about three percent predators and the balance prey, which live off vegetation. The herbivorous animals keep down the foliage, the predators keep down the grazing animals, and lack of prey keeps the predators' numbers in check."

"The residual effects of chaos?" asked Bernssen. "That's what governs this planet?"

"The weather tells us that much." Ralston rummaged about until he found the battered spear he'd used on the animal making its lair in the dioramas. He replaced the battery and tested the tip. A satisfying spark leaped off the steel tip.

He and Bernssen went back outside in time to see a hunched over creature stalking the broken ultrasonic digger.

"What is it?" whispered Bernssen.

"Whatever it is, it thinks the digger will be dinner."

Ralston moved forward to frighten off the creature, when it pounced. Strong claws ripped open the metallic siding of the digger, spilling wiring and circuitry to the cold ground.

"Damn!" roared Ralston, outraged. Without thinking,

he ran forward, spear in hand. The animal looked up. One emerald eye blazed with hatred. The other had been malformed, only a patch of fur where the socket should have been.

"Stop, Michael. Don't!" called Bernssen.

Ralston saw a precious piece of equipment being destroyed. While still recovering from his bout underground, he wasn't going to let this creature bring valuable work to a halt due to his own weakness. The creature swiveled about, one hind leg shorter than the other. Forepaws with glistening talons raked the air to hold Ralston at bay.

The professor feinted to the left, moved right and lunged. Just as the steel tip passed the creature's defending talons, Ralston hit the contact at the base of his spear. A jolt powerful enough to kill most animals this size jerked the creature back.

The potent shock hadn't even stunned it. If anything, it enraged the beast.

"Here, over here!" yelled Bernssen, waving his arms and trying to distract the creature. Only when the physicist threw a stone that bounced off the animal's misshapen skull did it turn.

Ralston saw his chance and acted. The spear flashed forward once more, this time finding a vulnerable throat. He didn't waste time with the switch. The nicked steel blade severed arteries. Blood spurting, the creature spun back to face Ralston.

On impulse, Ralston closed the contacts once more. This electrical surge flopped the creature onto its side. It lay there, feebly pawing the air. Bernssen came up, breathing hard and said, "Never saw anything like it."

"Look at its claws. They're metallic—naturally metallic. And the musculature. Such a powerful creature, but twisted out of shape."

"What spawned such a monster?" asked Bernssen.

"It's a mutant," said Ralston. "A mutant spawned by chaos."

Bernssen looked from the dead creature to Ralston and

back. The physicist swallowed hard. "We might be able to spare some extra time for you and Leonore," he said. And then, in a voice so low that Ralston barely heard it, Bernssen said, "I don't want my mother and sisters to *ever* see anything like that back on Novo Terra. Not ever!"

NINE

MICHAEL RALSTON SAT in his shelter, head cradled in his hands. For all the progress he'd made in finding the final refuge of the natives from Alpha 3, it had come undone. A dead end. There just wasn't anything more for him to find.

The excavation had been finished, in spite of the foul weather, in spite of the destruction wrought on the one digger, in spite of a dozen other vexing problems. Increasingly, they had been plagued with catastrophic equipment failures that Westcott attributed to the residual chaotic effect. The mathematician spoke of strange attractors and four-dimensional phase portraits and other terms so esoteric, Ralston followed not even the faintest of threads of the explanations given with such loving attention to rigorous detail.

"Michael?" came Leonore Disa's soft voice. "Are you all right?"

"No, dammit, I'm not," he snapped. "Why should I be? I've been mauled and beaten up and put through convulsions, and for what? Nothing. There's nothing here!"

"That's not so. We still haven't finished with the dioramas yet. There might be something in the few we haven't tried. Nels and I will start again early tomorrow morning." No conviction rang in her voice. She sounded as downcast as he felt.

"I know the contents of the last scene. I lived through it."

"We're gaining much more data," she said. "The anti-convulsant drug works well. Neither Nels nor I have experienced any ill effects from the scenes we've studied." She tried to put a bit of humor into her words. "It does make us a little sick to our stomachs, but that comes from my medport more than anything else."

"There's got to be something I'm missing. There must be. I *feel* it!" Ralston stood and began nervously pacing, hands clasped behind his back. "I'm not thinking this through. But what can be wrong? What is it I'm missing?"

"The city is completely excavated. Not much left, I'm afraid. The few artifacts don't give us any clearer picture of the Alpha 3 society than we'd already gotten."

"They lasted almost a hundred years. Dial and the others landed, and at least one generation of Alphans followed. But the chaos destroyed them, just as it had their planet. It must have worked on the embryo Alphans, and this decimated their birthrate. If only their culture had been more inclined to leave debris, garbage, something for us to study. All the Alphans seemed to have left of any consequence was their telepathic museum."

"Nels says the primary has quieted down. That's typical, though. Long stretches of intense solar storms followed by shorter plateaus of relative inactivity."

"The epilepsy," said Ralston, not listening to her. "There's that. Cancers. I'm sure their entire population was rife with it. The chaos field triggers oncogenes. Look at the hideously deformed creatures we've found. Those must have been native to Beta 5."

"You think they've mutated this rapidly?"

"Leonore, evolution is a rapid process, at least in a geologic sense. We're not talking millions of years to form those beasts, but a handful of thousands. The chaos device sowed its seeds of change all too well, I think."

"We're still likely to figure out how to duplicate the

telepathic projector," Leonore said. "That'll make the expedition seem better to Salazar, at least for us."

"This is really Bernssen's expedition. We just rode along. I need *more*. And there's something I've over-looked. Not the city. That was a dead end. The dioramas aren't giving us any more information than we either had or had guessed. What have I overlooked?"

Leonore shook her head. "Those seem to be the pertinent points, at least from an archaeology standpoint. Dial tried to leave as complete a record as possible, but they seemed to struggle too much just to survive. Querno died of an epileptic convulsion soon after they landed. Fennalt scavenged their spaceship to—"

"Fennalt!" cried Ralston. "That's it. I . . . I remember it now. In the last diorama. Dial detailed their troubles. He said that Captain Fennalt had settled on the far side of the planet hoping that this isolation would keep the chaotic plague from spreading."

"It obviously didn't."

"Get the satellite photos of the spot. Do it. Now!" he yelled. Leonore jumped at his tone. She took the hardcopy photos out and spread them on the table.

"So?" she asked.

"How extensive is the city on the far side of the planet? The one Fennalt settled?"

"Big," Leonore said, not sure what Ralston meant.

"Much bigger than this one, yet how many Alphans did Fennalt have with him? Only the ones they thought were untouched by the chaos—less than a hundred."

"You're saying they prospered and built the city? Verd, they may have lasted a generation or two longer, but they're gone, too. No trace of survivors anywhere."

"They weren't untouched. We know that. All who es-caped Alpha 3 carried with them the kernel for their eventual destruction, whether it was fast from epileptic seizure or slow from cancer. And they certainly found no relief on Beta 5—not with the chaotic effects running rampant among the animal population."

"I don't understand."

"Fennalt's group had no better chance to survive. And I don't think it did. Something Dial said—something in the diorama—went by me until now. I can't remember the exact words but the thought was that Fennalt had gone to colonize a city already constructed."

"Not by natives of Beta 5," said Leonore. She frowned. "We haven't found any trace of intelligent life anywhere else. Just those two spots. That's stretching logic to think that any natives would concentrate in one city, then just leave it for the Alphans."

"What if they weren't native to Beta 5? What if that was only a colony?"

"You mean another race colonized Beta 5, left, and then Fennalt moved in?"

"I have to start excavation at the other site. We've documented this one well enough. We can get our equipment crated and ready to move in a few days."

"But what about the dioramas we haven't activated!" Leonore protested.

"They're interesting, but only for details. *This* is new science. This is another find. Imagine, Leonore. We've found a planet that boasts *two* colonies. And the first ones to Beta 5 had to have space travel. Where else would they come from?"

"Inside the system or from outside?"

"How can we tell unless we work the site?" asked Ralston, smiling. Hope again rose within his breast. More of the Alphan culture might be revealed.

Ralston could hardly hold back the irrational hope at the idea that some of the Alphan refugees might have left Beta 5 with the builders of the colony. To speak directly to any survivor of Alpha 3 would prove invaluable. Not only could he check his guesses about their society, he might be able to learn exact details of the disaster that had befallen them.

He might learn everything about the chaos device.

•   •   •

"I don't like it, Leonore," Nels Bernssen said. The tall physicist slumped forward, a dour look on his face. "There's no way I can break off now and go with you. And changing our site is impossible. We've too much time and effort invested here." He straightened and almost shouted, "Dammit, why couldn't you have begun on the other site! Why change your mind now?"

Leonore hugged him tight and burrowed her face into his chest. "I don't want to go, Nels, but I have to. Michael can't work alone. Even with the cargo robots, one person can't set up a functioning dig."

"I can't let you take the supervisor. I need it to . . . to monitor the others." Nels' voice almost broke. Two of his team had developed cancers, one of the thyroid and another of the spleen. The automedic had painstakingly cured both, but Bernssen feared a virulent cancer might be beyond the small machine's capability. An undiagnosed pancreatic cancer might end a promising career and rob him overnight of a friend and colleague.

Even worse, from Bernssen's standpoint, was the potential for convulsive seizures.

"Keep the supervisor. We can get along without it. If there's just Michael and me—and maybe Westcott, if he decides to go—we won't need it. We can run one digger more efficiently using manual controls. The other equipment we can take out as needed."

"I don't want you to go," the man said simply.

"It's what I want to do. There's a good chance Michael is right. This might be another major find, a new alien site. Our job is to research other cultures by digging through their abandoned cities. I can't ask you to give up your work. Don't ask me to give up mine."

"I didn't say I wanted you to," Bernssen said. "I just meant that I'll miss you. With solar activity increasing the way it is, we might not be able to talk much, even using satellites."

"Set up one to relay microbursts. I can beam up as much as I want, the satellite will store it until it's overhead here, then you can retrieve it. The proton storms won't affect that much, will it?''

"I prefer holding you when I'm talking to you.''

"I know.'' Leonore Disa snuggled closer, but it soon came time to leave. Ralston waited impatiently for her. The pilot had returned with the landing pod to shuttle them halfway around the planet. This concession from the reclusive pilot wasn't to be dismissed lightly. Anger him and he might return to the starship still in orbit and not ground again on Beta 5 until they wanted to return to Novo Terra.

Leonore broke away and hurried outside, not daring to look back at her lover.

"This the place? Doesn't look like anything.'' The pilot's nimble fingers worked over the computer console. Ralston knew that the man had already programmed everything in; this was simply a show for the passengers.

"Mostly desert,'' said Ralston. "Land anywhere beyond the red rock upjuts. We want to stake out the site on the alkali plains.''

"Hard to call them plains. Look at the way the water's eroded them. Damn crazy weather on this planet. Can't tell from minute to minute what it's going to do.''

"This is unusual,'' pointed out Leonore. "The Alphans chose gently rolling land with grass and wooded areas nearby for their other cities. This is so . . . so different.''

"It reinforces the idea that someone else built it, doesn't it?'' said Ralston, peering into the viewscreen. His words abruptly cut off when the pilot touched down. The roar of rockets and the intense vibration jarred Ralston's teeth, and a momentary stab of pain went through his side. The automed had done a good job repairing the wounds inflicted by the mutant creature but deeper mending needed to be finished.

"We're down. I already got the laborobots working to uncrate for you. You want me to stick around for a while or get back into orbit?'' The pilot's tone made it obvious which he desired. Ralston made it easy on the man.

"Get us unloaded, then go on up. I want you to be able to pick either group of us up at a moment's notice."

"With the solar storms as bad as they are, you might be safer down here," said the pilot. But Ralston saw that the man preferred his lofty perch, no matter what the danger. "But all you need to do is call and I'll be here. Or give a flash if the radio transmission is out. You got the lasercom, don't you?"

Ralston looked to Leonore, who nodded. The cargo robot had unpacked their emergency communication unit first and had already checked it out.

"We're on our way. Thanks."

Ralston and Leonore clumsily left the shuttle and made their way through the slowly growing forest of crates. They had left most of their equipment at their first site with Nels Bernssen, but they still carried a great deal of mass.

"There's as good a site for camp as any," said Ralston, eyeing the terrain. A low sand dune would partially protect them when the shuttle launched; he might have chosen a spot farther away, but Ralston didn't want to take the time required to move the equipment.

"Mighty close," said the pilot, eyeing the choice critically. The man shrugged and turned back to the shuttle, not waiting for Ralston's answer. The pilot assumed Ralston knew the dangers—and like any other scientist, was absolutely insane.

Two hours later the shuttle launched. Ralston and Leonore Disa crouched behind a makeshift blast deflector. They hardly noticed the added heat from the shuttle pod's exhaust gases. The incessant winds blowing across the desert provided a natural kiln-hot environment. Shaking the dust and sand from their clothes, the two archaeologists stood and watched the contrail forming high above them in the clear azure sky.

"Makes you feel alone, doesn't it?" said Ralston.

"Verd," agreed Leonore. She shook herself again and

sent up a cloud of dust. "I hate this place. Let's get the digger going. The sooner we start, the sooner we leave."

"That's not the proper spirit," said Ralston, even though he shared her distaste for the desert. Like the Alphans, he preferred greener lands. Staying in the desert too long might even make him homesick for Novo Terra.

"I know. We go where the ruins are."

"You could have specialized," he told her. "The underwater excavation teams never have to deal with sand."

"No, just exterior pressures high enough to crush titanium hulls like paper. Funny air mixtures that make you squeak when you talk. Never being able to go for a nice long walk alone. I know all about the undersea people. They're crazy."

"They say the same about us," Ralston said. He bent to the task of pulling open the crates containing their digger while the laborobots put up plastic shelters to house them and the manually operated controllers. Four hours of work in the sun completed their camp.

"I've had it, Michael. I feel drained." Leonore collapsed onto her cot and hiked up her feet. She closed her eyes.

"We've done enough for the day. I wanted to get everything established. We'll work at night. Even with the sun only about half as bright as home, this heat is killing me." Ralston sighed and took a long, tepid drink of water already distilled by their precipitator. "Should have landed at dusk and worked in the evening to set up," he said. "Hindsight's always better."

"Not as good as sleep," murmured Leonore. In minutes, Ralston heard the woman's slow, even breathing.

The professor stared at her, wondering what drove her. She came from one of the richest families on Novo Terra. Why expose yourself to dirt, grit, and discomfort when you could be dining elegantly at the finest restaurants?

Ralston's thoughts turned to what drove him. He found this as unexplored an area of motivation in himself as in Leonore. The discovery of small pieces of information no one else had uncovered thrilled him, but was this the only reason he risked his life on a half-dozen different planets? It hardly seemed enough. Curiosity? Was it that simple? Ralston rolled it over and over in his tired brain, seeking the answer. Did he run from something or to it? The way he felt, he couldn't even walk.

He left Leonore's tiny plastic shelter and went to his own. He stretched out, tried to sleep, and couldn't; tiredness prevented it. His mind kept turning over and over what he hoped to find in these ruins. Dial *had* mentioned another race already here, but the Alphan had spoken so briefly of it that Ralston knew the ruins were ancient when the refugees landed on Beta 5.

The thought turned repeatedly in his head that the chance existed for some of the Alphans to be alive on some other world, that he might get closer to the mystery of the chaos device. It had ruined worlds, exploded stars, killed races, and hideously deformed creatures on Beta 5. As he drifted off into a sleep that was more like a coma, Ralston realized that he was interested in the refugee Alphans, he was interested in what might prove to be Betans, but his real desire for knowledge lay with the chaos field.

Was it a natural occurrence? A weapon? An accident? Had some race tried to contact others using it as a communication device? Why did it exist? Why?

"Over to your left. More, more, that's it." Michael Ralston signaled to Leonore to put the digger on a straight course. The ultrasonic broom spewed forth a miniature tornado of dust and white clay as it revealed the buried ruins.

The synthetic aperture radar had shown the buried structures, but it had failed to indicate their depth. It had taken a week of intense work to even reach the ruins. Ralston and Leonore worked in a pit almost four meters deep. The first meter had been the worst. Sand without anything to hold it poured into their excavation as fast as the digger removed it. Ralston had finally resorted to fusing the sand into glassy slag with a plasma torch.

After the first meter, work went faster until they struck a white caliche layer that continually overheated their digger. Water refused to soften the hard clay. Only patience worked. The final two meters had been relatively uneventful.

"We need a couple dozen others working with us," complained Leonore. Ralston saw that her nose was peeling from sunburn in spite of the medications she applied. Leonore had long ago turned off her jewelry plates; the water loss and sun-hardening of her skin, in spite of working at night, caused the plates' soft outlines to become more prominent. "Or a supervisor and a dozen diggers."

"We're getting there," said Ralston. He was hardly in better condition than his student. "But it is too bad Westcott didn't want to leave his computer. Imagine what he'd look like out here scrabbling through debris with his fingers."

The image of the mathematician doing anything but sitting in a chair and gazing glassy-eyed at infinity amused them both.

Ralson stayed on hands and knees following the digger as it unearthed the top of a building. The archaeology professor took photos of every trinket found, carefully tagged and boxed them, and kept on with the dreary work. The acquisition stage always dragged on interminably for him. He preferred the work of piecing together what they'd found, figuring out how the society had functioned, what the recovered oddiments were used for, *who* the people were.

"We need a sonic prober," he said. "This is a dome for a large building. From the curvature, it must be a good twenty meters in diameter."

"At least," agreed Leonore, standing to get a better look at the dome appearing under the digger's snout. "We'll have to put lights up higher to get a better look at it."

"What worries me is having to excavate over it if we want to expose it all. That's, hmmm, four meters deep and twenty diameter . . . almost twelve hundred fifty cubic meters."

"We might as well give up on that notion," said Leonore. She stared at the thirty-meter long, three-meter wide trench they'd dug. That had taken a week. The excavation Ralston threatened would require another month of hard work. Even then, they had no guarantee the effort would be rewarded.

"Can't figure out what this material is," said Ralston. "I'm actually considering using the torch to cut through it."

"That's sloppy archaeology. Do you really want to destroy what you've found?"

"Hardly, but we both know there won't be time for a real expedition. We don't have the equipment now, and the University isn't likely to send another group within a year. Nels said the sun's going to go nova some time after that, which would discourage most reputable University archaeologists."

"It didn't discourage us, either here or on Alpha 3."

"It'd discourage any *sane* archaeologist," he amended. Ralston continued to brush away the grit and the white clay with his hands while the digger worked ahead, removing the bulk of the sand. "Dammit! I'm so far gone I refuse to be stopped, by Chancellor Salazar or good sense or even chaos."

"And I'm with you!"

Ralston looked up. He had his answer. Leonore Disa had left Novo Terra for the same reasons he had. Unlocking the past held a lure more potent than any drug. To know things that others didn't, to present those facts, *that* was the addiction they shared.

"You're going to get committee approval on your thesis before long," he said. "If you ever finish it. You been working on it?"

"Michael!" she protested. "I've been spending every spare minute going over Beta material."

He shook his head in mock disapproval. "That's no way for a student to behave. The degree, that's the important thing."

"The work is," Leonore said flatly.

Ralston nodded, happy to hear her say it. She might be his graduate student, and he might be a political pariah at the University of Ilium, but he'd fight for her degree with the rest of her committee, with the entire department, if necessary. Leonore Disa was a good researcher and one of the best field investigators he'd ever seen.

"We're in luck," he said. "Look at this."

Leonore left the digger controls and stood above Ralston, looking over his shoulder. "What is it?"

"Don't know. It might be a hatch or a door. It seems to open by dropping down and then sliding to the side. Do you see any lock or opening mechanisms?"

"I'll direct the digger over and clear off a larger area. Maybe we can find the door bell."

A cracking sound echoed like thunder along their excavated trench. Ralston and Leonore exchanged glances.

"What was that?" she asked.

"It sounded like something breaking. Glass or . . ." Ralston's voice trailed off as he looked up at the sides of their trench. The areas where he'd fused the walls were starred with cracks.

"The trench is falling in. Get the—"

Ralson's words were cut off as an even louder crack sounded. The sandy walls of the trench collapsed, sending up dust clouds—and bringing down four meters of sand on top of them.

TEN

SHARDS FROM THE plasma torch-slagged trench walls shot past Michael Ralston's head like vitreous bullets. He ducked and felt himself being surrounded by the sand. Somehow, Leonore grabbed his arm. He pulled her close.

"Climb," he shouted. The rush of sand almost drowned out his command. But even as Ralston spoke, he knew that it wouldn't be possible. They were being swamped. The weight of the sand crushed him down to his knees, Leonore beside him.

Instinct for survival took over. He arched his back and strained mightily to keep from being driven flat onto the domed structure. With his arms outspread, Ralston managed to form a small cavity under his chest. But he found it increasingly difficult to maintain even this small breathing space as more and more of the sand piled on top of him and found its insidious way around his body.

"Michael!" cried Leonore. He sensed her wiggling around under him. "Hold on!"

"Trying," he panted.

Already the air turned stale. Less than a cubic meter of free space remained underneath his torso. Even as he panted and strained, sand poured around him, filling up this small space that gave them both a small hope for escape. Ralston began to black out. The pressure on his

111

back and shoulders overwhelmed him. His side began to ache, muscles ripping within his chest cavity. He tried to gasp in a lungful of air and got only sand. He choked. His strength began to fade, slowly at first, then with mounting speed.

"Leonore," he gasped, trying to tell her to get out from under him. She didn't hear; his voice failed. He crumpled onto her, the weight of the sand driving him down with manic fury.

For a moment, Ralston hung suspended in time and infinite space. His entire world had turned dark and sandy. His lungs strained and life ebbed from him.

He shrieked in surprise as he suddenly plummeted, the dome and Leonore no longer beneath him. Arms flailing as if he were a bird trying to fly, he fell through the air. He smashed hard into Leonore, his body atop hers.

Ralson lay stunned, not knowing what had happened. A tiny trickle of sand from above annoyed him. Then he laughed in delight. He could be annoyed. The compression of sand on his back had vanished. His lungs pulled in stale but breathable air. What was an hourglass trickle compared to that?

"Get off me, dammit," he heard Leonore say. The floor wiggled: Leonore.

"Sorry." Ralston moved slowly, painfully. The muscles in his side refused to give him anything but stabbing agony whenever he twisted. The professor tried to remain upright and not torque the damaged area. "What happened? We were trapped, then . . ."

Probing around with his hand, Ralston paused when he touched Leonore. They had fallen into the dome. That was the only possible answer. But if they'd found the front door, they had yet to discover the light switch.

"It's too dark to see anything," she said. "There must be lights, if we can find them."

"Let me catch my breath," he said, wincing at this small exertion. "What happened? How'd we get inside?"

"I found a depression in the dome just as the trench

walls caved in on us. I pressed down hard and the door worked. I didn't expect to fall so far, though. I think I broke my arm.''

"That makes me in better shape," lied Ralston. Every breath, now that he had sufficient oxygen, proved a trial. Knives of pain lanced into him each time he breathed in or out—and he wasn't up to holding his breath yet. Not after escaping a premature burial.

"You don't sound it."

"Help me up. We're going to have to explore. There's still sand coming down on my face. I don't think the door shut."

"It must have," she pointed out. "The entire dome would have been filled by now. Maybe the door only partially closed. That gives us time."

Ralston didn't ask time for what. He wanted to believe they could escape, but how they'd accomplish this miracle wasn't clear. Even if they turned on the lights, they were still in a dome buried under almost four meters of heavy sand. With his side injured again, and Leonore's arm broken, digging out using their hands didn't appear too attractive an option.

Edging slowly in the direction he faced, Ralston began his blind exploration. Several times he tripped over debris scattered on the floor, and once he took a nasty fall over a railing that caught him just below waist level.

"We can go on like this for years," complained Leonore. "We can starve to death doing it."

"I know. I'm hoping that we'll reach a wall soon. We can go around the entire circumference and get some idea what we have in the way of resources."

"After almost ten thousand years, you don't think the Alphans left anything useful, do you? Like a nice salad or even a few dried-out chocolate bars?"

"I just want to see where I am," he said. The mention of food caused his belly to grumble. For all his careful movement, Ralston slammed hard into the dome wall. The curvature had become more acute, allowing him to hit his head even though his probing foot and groping hand had found nothing.

"The wall?" Leonore asked eagerly. She tugged on his free hand as she worked around. In less than a minute they both squinted under the harsh light filling the huge dome.

Ralston held up a hand to protect his eyes until they adjusted. He realized that the light level was very low, far lower than an Alphan would find comfortable—and it was even dimmer than a Beta 5 twilight.

"I seem to have the knack for finding their controls," Leonore said proudly.

She had moved in precisely the right direction along the wall to find the lighting control panel. If they had gone in the opposite direction, they would have traversed over half the circumference before finding another switch. At least a dozen circular openings radiated from the dome, two of them between the archaeologists and the other light control. They might have blundered down one of those passages before finding the switch. Leonore's success almost made Ralston believe in luck.

"Let me look at your arm."

"What are you, an automed?" She winced as he gently probed. The simple fracture had to be set. Leonore gasped and almost fainted on him when he firmly grasped her wrist and elbow and exerted a steady pressure. He felt the bone snap into place just as the woman began to fight to get away from him.

"We'll find a splint for it somewhere, and you'll be all right again."

Tears ran down her cheeks and left dusty trails. "All right? How can you say that after you almost killed me?"

She looked up to the dome entrance, where sand still sifted past the door, then laughed. For a moment, Ralston looked at her, then he joined in until they clung to one another, laughing hysterically. Finally, sore and exhausted, the need for nervous release past, they sank to the floor of the dome and leaned awkwardly against the wall.

"What do you think this place was?" Leonore asked.

Ralston shook his head. "A storage area. A warehouse. Mostly, it looks unused by the Alphans. And the Betans didn't leave much."

He studied the sloping wall and the blister-shaped surface arching above them. The material appeared to be a tough plastic, but it had a metallic sheen to it that spoke of a different, otherworldly origin. The hatchway in the top of the dome wasn't intended to open into space as it had. Ralston saw points where a walkway had once been attached to the inner surface around the hatchway. For some reason, it had been taken down and the framework stored on the opposite side of the dome. Of a ladder or other way up he saw no trace.

"There's a corridor going into the rest of the complex," Leonore said. She cradled her right arm in her lap and used her left to point out the dark circular doorway.

"We're not going to find a way out sitting here."

They helped one another to their feet and started off, picking their way through the alien debris. Repeatedly, Ralston fought the urge to stop and study it. This wasn't merely garbage, it constituted an artifact left by an alien culture. As such, it held information. But he kept moving. While they were better off now than a short while ago, their lives still hinged on quickly finding a way out from under the crushing thousands of kilograms of sand.

"No lights," Leonore said. "We'll have to go slowly."

They edged down the tunnel. Ralston ran his hand along the sharply curved, smooth ceiling just a few centimeters above his head. The width didn't exceed two meters. The faint available light dimmed quickly. Luckily, they found the end of the tunnel before they floundered about in total dark.

"These are strange doors," Ralston remarked. "It's as if they pressurized the inside of the dome and connecting tunnels."

"Designed for a being used to living in a higher-pressure atmosphere?" Leonore asked.

"I can't think of any other reason for choosing the

interior designs. It gives me the sensation of being in a spaceship, the walls between me and a vacuum. But the atmosphere is a normal pressure for us, and very close for the Alphans."

The door to an airlock slid open slowly, its mechanism still functional after almost ten thousand years. Inside the chamber, Leonore found another light-control panel. Like the airlock and the other mechanisms, it, too, functioned perfectly. They entered a second, smaller dome. Ignoring the stale, dead air, the archaeologists looked around. This one had been outfitted with bars parallel to the floor and mounted just above eye level.

"The Alphans?" she asked. "They were avian. I'd never gotten any indication that they hung from perches, though."

"I never did, either, but most of what we know has been gathered in the dioramas. Those were intended to give specific history lessons, not an account of their day-to-day lives. We don't even know for sure what they ate."

Leonore looked around, shaking her head. "Whoever built the structure built it to last. Imagine buying anything on Novo Terra that'd last ten months, much less ten thousand years."

Ralston looked at the light source. "No filaments. No gas inside to leak out. I'm not sure how the light's produced, but it's a good guess that the light level and frequency hasn't changed much since it was installed. If we find out how the Betans did this, Salazar will jump through hoops again. Especially since it's an immediately marketable theft." His scorn for archaeology placed on such a basis was obvious, yet Ralston had a pragmatic side. He might not be liked or appreciated at the University of Ilium, but if he kept returning with profitable geegaws, his position, if not his often-denied tenure, was assured.

"Any culture that builds so solidly and well must be long-lived," said Leonore. "Even if we had the proper equipment, how would we determine the age? Take a chunk of the dome itself and check it out for radioactive decay?''

"That'd be one way," said Ralston. "But carbon dating is good for only about seventy or eighty thousand years. We might have to use fission-track dating, if we can find any uranium in the shell."

"You think this structure is *that* old? That technique will date back for billions of years."

"It's all guesswork. I doubt we'll be able to accurately date the structure, even if we had the time. We don't have any of the equipment for thorium-lead or potassium-argon series. We'd have to send it back to the University labs."

"And the entire system will be superheated plasma in a year or two," Leonore said dejectedly. "Why is it you can't make a discovery on a planet not at jeopardy?"

"It happens that way," Ralston said. "Live life at the edge and you're bound to fall off. My acquaintance with the chaos device has made it all the more likely I'm going to fail."

"The thought just occurred to me: Since the chaos field passed through this system, would *any* of the radioactive dating methods be accurate?"

"I'll have to ask Westcott," said Ralston. "It seems likely that decay mechanisms would change if subjected to an enforced randomness." He let out a long sigh. "It might even make elements not normally radioactive begin to kick out gamma rays."

Ralston fell silent as they examined the chamber. All that speculation might die with them unless they found a way to the surface. But in spite of the danger, Ralston found himself more and more engrossed in what they discovered about the Alphans' living arrangements in the Betans' abandoned colony.

Ralston had to call a break when his side began throbbing with pain strong enough to bend him over.

"Your ribs might be broken," Leonore said, a hint of sadism in her voice. She hadn't forgotten the way he'd jerked on her arm to reset the ulna. "Is there some way of bandaging you?"

"I'll be all right, if we can just get out of here. This looks more and more like a prison to me. Let's hope it doesn't begin to look like a coffin."

"They must have had ways out. The beings that build so sturdily wouldn't risk being trapped by a sandstorm."

"That doesn't follow," he pointed out, his mind working on the problem. "If they were higher pressure beings, they wouldn't venture outside much. It wouldn't matter to them if they were buried under a kilometer of sand or sat on the surface." Ralston moved to a more comfortable position. "They had to have built on the surface, though. The four meters we dug through are the result of chaotic storms over the years since the Alphans came."

"The Alphans wouldn't have wanted to be buried."

"The storm patterns might not have been the same then. Or they might have excavated. . . ." Ralston paused and thought for a moment. He and Leonore exchanged glances.

"No, I didn't shut it off. I didn't have time," Leonore said.

"Then the ultrasonic digger is still working above us." Hope flared. "It had been programmed to clean off the stretch of dome around the hatchway, and it doesn't care if it's buried or not. It burrows as well as it sweeps."

"Then all we have to do is get back up to the hatchway and get the digger as it comes across. We can direct it upward."

"That's a lot of digging—and don't forget, the sand will come rushing in when we open the hatch."

"We can figure out something," Leonore said, dismissing this. "It might be harder for us to get back to the hatch. The ladder's gone and the walkway has been junked."

Ralston remembered the drop; they had fallen almost six meters.

"We can stack up debris," he said, looking around. It would be hard, but he thought they had enough to make a tottering mountain. "We might have to scavenge the entire complex, but I want to look through it, anyway."

"There must be ladders or climbing apparatus stored somewhere," Leonore agreed.

The two left the chamber where they thought the Alphans had slept. A tunnel leading to another, smaller dome, seemed to be the pattern followed throughout the buried complex. The central dome through which they'd tumbled provided a hub for the outstretched tunnels, the body of an octopus throwing out its tentacles.

Hours later, after they had separated and explored independently, they reunited. Ralston and Leonore sank to a low uncushioned bench made from the same material as the dome.

"No dioramas," Leonore said in disgust. "I'd hoped to find one telling all about this place."

"The Alphans were desperate and under immense strain when they established this outpost. Most of their equipment and expertise remained at the other site."

"It didn't do them any good. There aren't even any bodies."

"I gathered some dust that might be organic. I put it in a specimen envelope. When we get back, we can run some tests on it to determine the source." He looked at a small bag Leonore dragged behind her. "What's in that?"

"I don't know. I found it in a small room at the far end of the third tentacle-corridor. The room looked like an office, but it didn't have any furniture in it. Hardly any furniture anywhere, for that matter."

Ralston rummaged through the bag and came out with a stack of shiny disks. He held one up to the wan light and studied it.

"This might be a primitive laser recording," he said. "You didn't see any equipment?"

Leonore shook her head tiredly.

"I didn't, either. There's no hint to the original owners of this fine property," he said. "But I did find a room filled with stanchions and spare paneling. If we can get it up to the hatchway, we might be able to build a dam to keep the sand from pouring in.''

"And from there we can get the digger and burrow for the surface." Leonore's face had a pinched, drained, white look to it. Ralston realized the strain she was under—the strain they both felt so acutely. He was in charge of this expedition and he had let down his student, endangering her life in unprofessional ways. Worse, he had to continually fight to keep from rubbing his stomach to quell the growls of hunger.

But Ralston had one advantage over Leonore. He had been hungry before, many times before. Back on a burned-out Earth he had often gone days without any food and only a thin, dirty trickle of water to provide a small measure of liquid. And again, during the Nex-P'torra war, he had almost starved until he found which of the Nex foods suited him and which didn't. None of their warships had been equipped for aliens.

Ralston chuckled when he thought of the food he'd managed to get aboard to supplement the Nex rations. To this day he shuddered at the memory of peanut butter eaten to the exclusion of all else. But even this wouldn't go down badly, he thought.

"Let's get to work," he said. "The sooner we get out of here, the sooner we can eat." He watched in concern as Leonore got to her feet and wobbled. She caught herself and pretended it hadn't happened. Ralston tried to remember how long it had been since they'd eaten.

A day? Even if it had only been a few hours, they'd been through much. The strain of survival burned calories quickly.

"Bring that bag with you. It's got about all this place has to offer in the way of artifacts."

Leonore listlessly dragged it behind her into the main dome.

Ralston, in spite of his injured side, did more of the heavy work. Leonore's right arm lacked strength. It took only a few minutes for him to see how much it still pained her. He dragged the panels and beams into the room while she worked out a system for getting them the necessary distance to the overhead hatchway.

"It'll be shaky, but bracing one beam there, lifting and bracing another against it like this, and then dragging the panels up one sloping side is the easiest," she said, sketching out the blueprint in the sand beneath the still-leaking hatch.

"Let's do it."

Ralston started and, with Leonore's help, they built the rickety structure in less than an hour. It took him another two to get the panels up and in place.

"I can hear the digger working," he said, shouldering a panel into position. The cofferdam seemed ready.

They looked at one another. In their weakened condition, they had done all they could. If only they'd had their full excavation equipment with them!

"Ready?" asked Ralston.

Leonore nodded. She edged along the beam and found the inner lock mechanism. Ralston readied himself to force the paneling through the hatchway when it slid open.

"Now!" she cried.

The hatchway slid open, and Ralston shoved with all his strength to lift the cofferdam into the imprisoning sand.

He knew instantly that he'd misjudged both the weight of the sand and his own strength. The makeshift wedge shifted to one side and Ralston was unable to hold it. The rush of sand drove him backward along the narrow platform they'd constructed.

Torrents of choking sand rushed to fill the dome.

ELEVEN

"NO!" SHRIEKED LEONORE DISA. "Stop it! Don't let it come in!"

Michael Ralston had no way of stopping the torrent of crushing sand. It bowled him over, sending the pitifully inadequate cofferdam in one direction and him in another. He clung onto the platform brace and watched as the cascading sand took his laboriously constructed panels to the floor of the dome and immediately covered it. He spat and fought to get the sand from his eyes. Side hurting terribly, he got back to his feet and joined Leonore.

Less than two meters away the sand rushed noisily into the dome in a torrent so powerful that the best excavation equipment couldn't have halted it.

"We're going to die," Leonore said in a voice totally calm. "The sand will fill the dome and we'll die. We can't even reach any of the branching corridors."

Ralston shielded her with his body, but the choking sand flew everywhere. He pulled off his shirt and tore it into strips. He and Leonore breathed through the sweat-stiff fabric, but this did little to furnish clean air to his lungs or to stop the polar coldness in his gut from spreading. He had heard the woman's dire words; he knew they were true.

123

All they could do was stand on the rickety platform and wait for death.

"What's that?" Leonore asked. "Something's wrong."

Ralston almost laughed at this. Everything had gone wrong. Then he heard the curious, unexpected sound, too. It was almost as if the deafening rush of sand diminished. Squinting, he turned and peered into the dust.

"It's stopping. I don't know why, but it's stopping!"

In less than a minute the torrent had reduced to a trickle. Ralston, curious, edged over. Leonore followed closely. He peered up through the hatchway and saw the ultrasonic digger humming away as it cleared a spot on the dome's surface.

"The digger?" asked Leonore, incredulous.

"No, not entirely," said Ralston, suddenly realizing what had happened. "When the hatchway opened, the loose sand that had collapsed on us came rushing in. When a cone shape formed, the edges of the sand cone poured through, but soon after an equilibrium was formed. Getting out will be hard since we have to climb the sloping walls of a sandpit, but we can breathe! And the sky!"

"I'd thought Nels had come to see why we hadn't reported in," she said in a low voice. Then, brighter, "I never thought such dry desert air and hot sun would look good."

"You first," Ralston said. He boosted her up, wincing at the sharp pain in his side. He stood wobbling as Leonore kicked her way through the hatch and onto the small area the digger worked persistently to keep free of sand.

"We can make it, Michael. The climb won't even be that hard. Do you need help?"

"Get some rope and tie it around the digger's frame. Let it pull me out," he said. Ralston didn't want to admit to her that he wasn't able to follow.

"That'd mean going back to camp. I'm not sure I can make it up the slope without help. Here."

He heard ripping noises. In a few minutes a tattered rope made from her blouse dropped in front of him. He hefted the bag containing the disks Leonore had found, secured them to his belt, tied a bowline in the cloth rope, and fitted himself inside the loop.

"Pull away!" he shouted.

The digger almost didn't have enough power to lift him. But with Leonore's one-handed aid, he managed to get free of the dome without fainting from the pain. He lay on the sandy surface and shook. They had cheated death too often since arriving. This alien structure had almost become their tomb.

"I don't want to stay here. I want to get back to camp, where I can take a bath. It doesn't even matter that it's a chemical one." Leonore stood bare to the waist.

"You're going to sunburn," Ralston said. He sat and stared at her. She wasn't beautiful, but Ralston wasn't sure he had ever seen anyone more attractive.

"Do you gawk or do you climb?" she asked indignantly.

"Climb, but the gawking isn't such a bad choice."

Together they made their way up the shifting, treacherously yielding slope of the land. They finally flopped flat on the sunbaked surface and looked down into the cavity.

"I'd heard about insects on Earth that trap their prey using this arrangement," he said. "Ant lions, I think they're called. The ant slips down the side. When it tries to climb out, the ant lion begins digging under the ant's feet. When it tires, it slides all the way to the bottom, where the predator eats it."

"I'm glad you told me about that now," Leonore said, looking at the bottom, where the digger worked to hold back the inevitable cascades of sand.

They helped one another back to their shelters. Ralston wanted nothing more than to collapse. Without undressing he fell onto his cot. Nearby, he heard Leonore cursing as she clumsily worked to take a chemical bath. Ralston fell asleep, happy to be alive.

"You didn't make yourself look very clever," said Nels Bernssen, looking over Ralston's shoulder as the archaeology professor finished his weekly report. "In fact, when Salazar gets this, he'll have you up on charges."

"That'd be nothing new," said Ralston. He leaned back, free of pain at last. The automedic had worked on him for three days, then given him sedation for another three. Even though he hadn't broken any ribs, Ralston wondered if it might not have been better if he had. The muscle tears refused to heal quickly. Long after Leonore's broken arm had been returned to use, he had still moved with some difficulty and often considerable pain.

"You don't have to be so . . . frank."

Ralston looked up at the physicist. "This is what happened. I'm not going to alter the truth just to make myself look better. I know others do it." Ralston's mind produced a list of a half dozen just in the archaeology department at the University who had been overly creative in their reports to avoid problems with both University officials and protective parents. "Who knows? This might give us a real clue to the Betans. If I tried to make myself look less like an idiot, that might hide the facts we need."

"Still, Michael, there're ways of telling the truth without it being so masochistic. What's wrong with saying you thought about it, then logically figured out how to escape from the dome, rather than saying what happened was both accidental and unplanned and that you hadn't intended to get out that way?"

"Nothing, but it didn't happen that way. 'Hard are the ways of truth, and rough to walk.' "

"What?"

"A friend of mine is a medieval lit prof. Some of it must have rubbed off. That's from Milton."

"Milton who?"

"What's going on with the primary? How're your experiments coming along?" Ralston asked, changing the subject. Bernssen's expression turned to one of concentration.

"Good. We're able to find more pronounced pre-nova conditions in the Beta star than we did in the Alpha. My theory is working out well. The only trouble is equipment failure. Westcott says it's due to the chaos field's residual effects.''

"I want to fission-track date the dome and other artifacts we found, but I'm afraid that the chaos field might have affected the rate of radioactive decay. Did Westcott say anything about being able to correct for this?''

"We've been talking a great deal about the fusion process in the primary. I can't say I like him much, but I'll give the hijo this—he knows his math. That question came up. He showed me how a rapid passing of the chaos field wouldn't affect radioactive decay.''

"Why not?'' Ralston frowned. He wasn't a physicist but it seemed logical to him that if people developed neural problems and computer components failed, the radioactive decay process would be similarly afflicted.

"All nuclear processes are reversible. If the field forced an alpha decay, for instance, it also changed the probabililty for an alpha collision into the stripped nuclei.''

"So we're getting as much change in decay as we are in creation?'' Ralston worried over this. It didn't seem right.

"We'd never be able to observe the difference,'' Bernssen said with confidence. "It's like the Doppler shifting on stars. We talk about red shift if the object's moving away and blue if it's coming toward the observer, but the human eye still sees the star as its original color. *All* the spectrum is shifted, so the components that were in either IR or UV are brought into the visual, depending on the direction of the shift. Instruments can pick it up because the characteristic spectral lines are shifted, but the eye is happy.''

Ralston had trouble even figuring out the operational theory behind his automated excavation equipment. This had the ring of truth to it but lay beyond his expertise.

Leonore interrupted before he could work out the logic.

"Michael, Westcott wants to see you. It's about the disks.''

"Disks? Oh, the artifacts you found in the dome. What about them?'' Ralston had another page to write before the weekly report was finished. And, although he didn't want to tell her, the luxury of simply sitting and not moving seemed more valuable than finding what the computer-connected mathematician had to say.

"It's important. You might want to come, too, Nels."

Ralston heaved himself up and switched off his recorder. No pain. He appreciated that more than he had in the past. Maybe he should try to placate Salazar and the others and stay at a nice, safe, injury-free teaching post. As quickly as the thought crossed his mind, he rejected it. Ralston wouldn't become like Pieter Nordon, content to lecture and live off past glories. Nordon only put in time until retirement; he no longer did research.

As far as Ralston was concerned, Nordon had already retired—died—and didn't know it.

The trio went to Westcott's shelter. From inside the plastic shell came the dull, almost infrared glow that Westcott preferred when he linked to his computer. In a way, it reminded Ralston of the illumination inside the alien dome.

"Close the damned door," Westcott grumbled. "Too much light confuses my sensory link."

The three said nothing. Westcott would get to his discovery when it suited him and not a second before. The mathematician swung around on his hard chair and pointed.

"Those are recording disks. A form of laser disk, but very primitive. We must leave the surface of this planet immediately."

Ralston recovered first and asked, "Why? Are those the records of their last days? What happened to them?"

"What? They left. They got bored. I can understand that. They didn't seem to have computers, at least not good ones. No, they had none at all. None. Odd." Westcott shivered at the very idea of a culture not using the device he found so vital to his research.

"You're referring to the Betans?"

"Call them what you will. They colonized, put down the remote post in the desert, then decided against maintaining it, so they went back home."

"Where?" demanded Bernssen. "In this system? If it

is, we've got to locate them soon and warn them about the sun. A year or two is little enough time to leave a research facility. For an entire planet's population—"

"Wait, Nels," cut in Leonore. "We didn't detect radio transmission from any of the four sunward planets. And the three outer ones are gas giants."

"They left for the outer moon," said Westcott, ignoring the debate raging around him. "They had used it as a stepping-stone. Their main base was located there. The one you found in the desert," he said, looking at Leonore with some scorn, "was only a minor outpost. A trifle, a curiosity and nothing more."

"Moon?" asked Bernssen. "The moon orbiting this planet?"

"Where else?" the mathematician said, irritated. "These disks hint that they hollowed it out, then lived within it."

Bernssen muttered to himself and left without another word.

"There might be artifacts left on the moon—in the moon," Ralston corrected. His heart beat faster as the possibilities came to him. Digging out the dome on the far side of the planet constituted a chore he didn't want to think about. Even with full-scale equipment and enough personnel to do the work, it'd be a tedious process and one hardly worth the effort.

Deep down, he thought he and Leonore had scoured the inside of the dome complex as well as if they'd taken their time, used proper archaeological procedures, and had photographed everything in detail as they went. The recording disks had been the true find—and the light source for the interior of the dome provided a possible cash return for the expedition that would suit the bureaucrats back on Novo Terra. Ralston knew they could always burrow back into the dome to study the lighting system and the metallo-plastic walls.

The idea of a new base inside the moon orbiting Beta 5 excited him more. Such an outpost might hold more artifacts, perhaps even star charts to indicate the home planet

of those he called Betans. And Ralston couldn't deny the
fervent hope on his part that the Betans had observed the
passage of the chaos device. They had to be more experienced and sophisticated space travelers than the Alphans to
establish such a durable base on another planet. The Alpha
3 refugees had fled their home world through necessity.
The Betans were explorers, and probably disciplined, ac-
complished scientists.

Ralston glanced at Leonore, who nodded and smiled
broadly. Her thoughts paralleled his.

"We're going to check out the moon. What else did you
find in the disks?"

"They said nothing useful. Meanderings on shuttle schedules, manifests, things like that." The mathematician care-
lessly tossed one of the disks onto his cot.

Ralston didn't quite dive after it, but the urge proved
hard to deny. They had blundered across an archaeologist's dream. To know the daily schedules and concerns of
the Betans could be as significant as finding the Domes-
day Book.

"It did set me off on another, rather elegant proof,
however," continued Westcott. "This is the first opportunity I've had to see alien records. Their lack of computer
encoding interested me, even though the data were entered
in a binary code." Westcott sat with eyes closed, hands
crossed over his belly. The IR sensor atop his head pulsed
slowly as it linked with the computer across the room.

"What's your problem?" asked Leonore. Ralston shot
her a sharp look. The mathematician failed to understand
or take offense at the double entendre.

"It's been shown repeatedly that all computer languages
are equivalent, that none is in any way ultimately superior
to another. These trinkets suggest to me another proof that
is more universal than the others presented. This will
create a stir, yes, it definitely will. And it is so elegant, so
brilliant."

"The disks," pressed Ralston. "What about them?"

"I don't need them any longer. They've served their

purpose. But I do want to accompany you when you explore the moon. That can present all manner of new problems to solve.'' Westcott actually cackled and rubbed his hands together. ''This expedition is providing me with data that'll take years to work through. What a bonanza!''

''We feel the same way, Dr. Westcott,'' Leonore solemnly assured the mathematician. Before she could say anything more, Bernssen opened the door of the shelter and motioned silently. Both archaeologists left to join Bernssen outside.

''This son of a bitch is right. *Madre de Dios!*'' Muttered Bernssen. ''I ran a quick check on the orbital dynamics of the outer moon. It couldn't possibly be solid. It's nothing more than a hollow shell. We should have discovered that, not him!''

Leonore laid her hand on Bernssen's shoulder. This didn't seem to soothe him.

''Westcott expects us to go check out the moon. For once, I have to admit he has a good point.'' Ralston shook his head. ''There might be more than a little scientific curiosity lurking within him, in spite of the computer linkage.''

''I used the lasercom to get a beam up to the pilot. Even though he's not too happy with us—claims we're using him as a taxi service, first to one side of the world, then back—he'll be landing at dawn tomorrow. We're going to have to consider conserving fuel on the shuttle now, after all these up and down trips. I don't think there's need for more than the three of us to go.''

''And Westcott,'' added Ralston. ''He's proving himself useful, even if getting information out of him is like drawing blood.''

''We just don't talk the same language,'' said Bernssen. He smiled wryly. ''And I thought I was good at math. Westcott lives in a different geometry from this universe.''

''The four of us will go. Some equipment, but not much. I don't want to spend the rest of my life packing and unpacking. Cameras, some analysis equipment, a few robot probes.''

''Michael,'' Leonore said gently, ''I know what we'll need.''

Ralston nodded absently and left, walking off into the newly forming rainstorm to think about all that Westcott had discovered. He might not like the less-than-human mathematician, but he couldn't deny that he'd done a considerable amount of good work for the expedition.

An entire moon filled with artifacts! A new chance to find the source and destination of the chaos device awaited him. The fate of the Alphans, the home of the Betans, those were promised him, too.

Michael Ralston could hardly restrain himself until take-off the next morning.

TWELVE

"It CAN'T BE done. I refuse to commit suicide for you fools." The pilot grumbled even more under his breath, only faint static noises reaching Ralston and the others in the passenger compartment of the starship.

"Can we use the shuttle to land on the moon?" asked Nels Bernssen. "The maneuver won't be too hard, and it's similar to landing on the surface of Beta 5."

"No, it's not," snapped the pilot. "You can't orbit this son-of-a-bitch moon. Too small for that. Too small for any of the damned things you plan to do."

"It's not too small," said Westcott. "Why is he saying that? I can show mathematically that we have ample room to maneuver, and of course it is always possible, if not desirable, to orbit another celestial body. The diameter of this particular moon is, of course, smaller than either of the moons circling Novo Terra, but this has nothing to do with the shuttle landing on the surface."

"He's mad at us," said Ralston. "We've disturbed him for a third time."

"It's his business to move us from one spot to another," Westcott said, almost primly. The sensor mounted on top of the mathematician's head winked on and off slowly. Ralston decided it must have been put on standby since they were out of line-of-sight for any of the on-board computers or linkups.

"We'll handle it," said Leonore. She flipped around neatly in free fall and faced the vidscreen. "Please, we do so need to land. It's *very* important for us."

Bernssen snorted in disgust. To Ralston he said in a low voice that didn't carry any farther, due to the low air pressure in the ship, "She always gets what she wants when she uses that tone of voice. Works every time on her father." The physicist snorted again. "Works every time on me."

Ralston smiled when he felt the steering jets on the ship kick in. The starship rolled slightly as it oriented itself in orbit. In the vidscreen he saw the pilot beginning the maneuver that would place them in position to launch the shuttle.

"I'm putting the ship into a figure-eight orbit around the moon and the planet," the pilot said with ill grace. "That means I can only rendezvous with you every third day."

"Not so," said Westcott. "The actual calculations show that—"

Bernssen shut up the mathematician before he angered the pilot further. "Let's get into the shuttle, why don't we, Dr. Westcott?" Bernssen asked, pulling the man along like a captive balloon. Ralston saw that the physicist had to restrain himself from grabbing the IR sensor unit and using that as a convenient handle.

Ralston no longer cared about the petty squabbles between mathematician and pilot. Pilots were notoriously difficult to deal with, and Westcott's unnatural direct linkage with a computer had turned him into something other than human. Ralston's real interest focused on the second vidscreen and its telescopic display of the outer moon's dusty surface. Some medium-size cratering was evident, but not as much as Ralston would have thought.

"The moon rotates slowly, once every 448 hours," said Bernssen as they drifted along the narrow access corridor toward the shuttle airlock. "When I checked my figures, it became apparent that it isn't as massive as it should be if it were solid. Moments of inertia and all that. Should have been more careful. With that sort of information you and Leonore could have explored here first."

"Now is as good a time as any. If we find the proper location, do you think you would want to set up an observatory? It'd be clear of Beta 5's atmosphere."

"Actually, that's been proving helpful, having an atmosphere," Bernssen said. "It filters out the worst of the solar storms. The planet's magnetosphere captures the ionized particles, and I've always found it easier to work with a near-normal gravity. Some of the men, though, prefer zero-g or near-g. The moon'll only give us about ten percent what we're used to."

"Would those solar storms have damaged anything inside?" Ralston asked, the possibility of finding nothing but fried artifacts not suiting him at all. He'd come too far to lose out again. Alpha 3 had been ripped away from him in the cataclysmic explosion of a nova. Beta 5 would be taken sooner or later, too, before he could mount a proper expedition and carefully document the most significant of his finds. To not even have the opportunity of digging through meaningful debris of this unknown alien culture irritated him.

"Getting radar returns from the moon," came the pilot's voice. He sounded almost cheerful.

Leonore looked questioningly at Ralston, who only shook his head. He had no idea what amused the pilot about standard procedures.

"Buckle up. We're going down," said Bernssen. Leonore slid into the co-pilot's seat beside him. He frowned but said nothing as he began to look over the instruments. The pilot had programmed the on-board guidance computer. All they had to do was sit inside the shuttle and go along for the ride.

Ralston watched as Bernssen made a few minor adjustments. Leonore waited for the physicist to finish, then changed the controls back to their original reading. Ralston wondered at the relationship between his graduate assistant and Bernssen. He suspected Leonore was a competent enough pilot, but Bernssen obviously didn't know. Why hadn't she told him?

To pass the time while he awaited the sharp acceleration from the shuttle rockets, Ralston worked over the problem as if it were one of archaeological importance. Leonore Disa came from a very wealthy family; Ralston knew nothing of Nels Bernssen's background, but he didn't seem to be rich. Everyone on Novo Terra was well enough off so that no one starved, but most lacked the substantial wealth of a Disa family. Was Leonore holding back some of her talents to keep from hurting Bernssen's ego? Ralston considered this and decided it might be true. Bernssen had found fame with the chaos-induced nova of the Alpha primary, but researchers seldom got wealth along with their notoriety. Leonore might be keeping back some of her skills—such as piloting a starship or shuttle—because that accentuated the differences in their backgrounds. Most people never left Novo Terra, much less had the money or opportunity to use a private starship.

Such deception, or at least lack of honesty, on Leonore's part surprised Ralston. He had to consider that she worked conscientiously and well in the field when it came to scientific matters but operated under a different set of rules in her personal life. Leonore was no tri-vid beauty, but Ralston had always heard it said that money was the perfect aphrodisiac. What did the woman have to contend with as she grew up? Fortune seekers?

Whatever else Nels Bernssen was, Ralston got no hint of avariciousness in the man. His dedication to his work was foremost. In fact, that dedication almost amounted to monomania, something with which Ralston could identify. Nothing thrilled Ralston more than the beginning of a dig, the first find, the piecing together of the information to create a coherent whole culture. Bernssen's excitement over the chaos field and its effects rivaled his own.

It was good that Leonore shared such devotion. They

wouldn't have much common ground otherwise, Ralston decided. And the woman wouldn't have anything in common with Bernssen, either.

"Any way we can make a few circuits around the moon before grounding?" asked Ralston. "I'd like to get a close-up view of it. Take a few photos and—"

The acceleration shoved him back into his couch. Over the vibration of the rockets, Leonore called out, "We can't. We're going straight in. We have to conserve fuel for the shuttle. Too many trips back and forth to Beta 5 already."

Ralston cursed. He knew she was probably right. The pilot hadn't been speaking out of irritation over the extra work when he said they were getting low on shuttle rocket fuel. Without the laser launchers used on Novo Terra and other planets, fuel mass became a real economic consideration.

"Picking up extraneous signals on the radar," said Bernssen. "Leonore, do you recognize the pattern?"

Ralston saw her shake her head. Short brown hair flew in all directions as the rockets momentarily cut off and let them coast. As suddenly as the free fall had come, the acceleration again seized him. The shuttle touched down on the surface of the moon. On the screen Ralston saw huge clouds of grey-brown dust rising around them. The computer instantly cut rocket blast, but the cloaking veil continued to rise. In the moon's low gravity, it might be hours before it settled again and allowed them a clear view of the surface.

"I don't know what to make of it," Leonore said. "We're picking up a radar signal. Not a return but a new signal."

"Not from the starship?" asked Ralston.

"From the horizon. That's in the wrong direction for the pilot to reach us," she said.

Ralston looked at her, thought about their situation, then felt a momentary pang of guilt. His excitement at what this meant was undeniable. A radar pulse meant that the Betans had left a beacon, and their approach had somehow activated it after all these millennia. New sites to sift through, a new culture to bring from the depths of time to the bright light of scientific scrutiny. Ralston's guilt came from this selfishness on his part.

Leonore Disa was his student, and he was responsible for her advancement. She had applied for a doctorate, and every new discovery put her that much further away from fulfillment of the requirements. How could anyone keep from following the intriguing threads of Beta culture? Yet Leonore needed to concentrate on one aspect—of the Alpha 3 society—and do a thesis. Without direction, without narrowing her sights to a single topic, she might drift along, forever doing research and not finishing her degree requirements.

And Ralston was responsible for her lack of diligence in pursuing her degree. He continually dangled new and ever more enticing puzzles before her. Anyone with scientific curiosity had to follow. It was his academic responsibility to stop her from going in all directions, get her oriented properly, complete the degree and *then* explore the new clues to a different alien society.

But time! Ralston cursed the arrow of time piercing his schedules. The chaos device had shaken up all Ralston's perspectives. The Alpha primary had gone nova. Bernssen said the Beta sun would follow soon. Time crushed in from all sides.

"Michael, are you all right?" she asked.

"Oh, verd, yes, fine, fine." Ralston shook himself and swung out of the acceleration couch. He tottered for a moment as he adjusted to the slight gravity. "Let's find that radar beacon," he said, picking up a camera and a half-dozen floater probes.

"From the first contact and the one now," said Bernssen, "it must be about four kilometers toward the low hills." He pointed, but the direction made no difference to Ralston. He had no sense of a north or any other direction.

Westcott sat on the edge of his couch with a distant look

in his eyes. The slow blinking of the red indicator light on his IR sensor gave the only hint that the man still lived. Even his breathing seemed to have ended.

"What's wrong?" asked Ralston, knowing how the mathematician hated to be disturbed, and not caring. If Westcott's been injured in the descent, Ralston wanted to see him attended to before they left.

"Signals. The entire moon comes . . . alive. We have set off a chain reaction. I can't understand it. Any of it. The computer senses, yet it doesn't. There is too little to compute properly. I don't understand." Westcott put his head in his hands. Ralston thought for a moment that the mathematician had begun to cry, but Westcott looked up with dry, wide eyes. "I'm frightened," he said in a low voice that chilled Ralston more than if Westcott had screamed it.

"Of what, Dr. Westcott? The radar beacon signal? Something was activated?" Leonore obviously didn't share Westcott's fear. She already worked to don her spacesuit.

Westcott couldn't answer. Ralston helped the mathematician to his feet and started getting into his own suit. In less than fifteen minutes they had fastened the last of the web straps and collected the equipment they'd need. Ralston nodded to Bernssen, who cycled open the airlock. Only a tiny hiss sounded in Ralston's ears, then nothing. They looked out across the dust-shrouded surface of the moon.

The four of them unloaded the remainder of the equipment they needed for a preliminary reconnaissance and started toward the low hills and the radar beacon. Ralston alone of the four felt comfortable in the spacesuit. He led the way through the tumbled, jagged rocks and heavy dust. In less than twenty minutes they emerged from the cloud of dust stirred by their landing. In another twenty they had reached the base of the hills.

Ralston turned up the volume on his suit com and spoke to Bernssen. "Where do we go up?"

Bernssen looked back at the stubby shuttle sitting in the middle of the plain, checked his inertial tracker, then pointed off at an angle. Bernssen and Ralston looked up the slope, and Leonore might have, too. But not Westcott.

From the mathematician came a choked sound. He stumbled forward, still unused to moving in low gravity and spacesuit. "Here. It's here. But what is it? I can't think fast enough to find out. What is it? Oh, why can't I be faster, like my computers?"

The moan of frustration and fear brought the other three around. Ralston saw the source of Westcott's reaction. A small circular cut of decidedly artificial origin opened into the hillside. The four advanced slowly. Ralston photographed as he went, and Leonore took one of the robot probes from his pack. She moved it around so that he could see the settings she made.

"Think this is too far?" she asked. She had set it to fly five hundred meters down the dark corridor, then return.

"Let's try it and see what happens."

She triggered the probe. It vanished silently, to return in less than five minutes. Leonore plugged in the reader and studied the abbreviated output, telling what the probe had discovered.

"Well?" demanded Bernssen, obviously uneasy now. Ralston saw that Westcott's barely controlled panic affected them all, the astrophysicist most.

"Nothing. Just a smooth-walled tunnel. There's some indication of a door another hundred meters deeper. Nothing to indicate weak walls or ceiling, no pits, side tunnels or . . ."

"No traps," finished Westcott. "This is a dangerous place. I . . . I feel it. They did not build this for us. No, not for us."

"You don't have to go with us," said Ralston. "It might be better if you stayed behind. We'll want to be able to relay back to the shuttle and to the pilot if anything happens. If we all went into the tunnel, it might cut off radio transmission."

"I can't stay here and simply wait," said Westcott, almost in a panic. "I have to go in. Don't you see,

Ralston? This might hold the key to it all. All of it! I can't let it frighten me off. I couldn't live with myself if I did!''

"The key to what, Dr. Westcott?" asked Leonore.

"The chaos equations. I *see* them in my head all the time. Their solution is so close. If I can only get the key, the one elegant masterstroke that will allow it to fall into place. What causes the bifurcation in the parameters? I need to know that or nothing makes sense.''

"The answer is inside?" asked Bernssen. He stood a pace away, as if afraid that Westcott's insanity might be contagious, even through the spacesuits. He dealt with men and women whose genius placed them perilously close to insanity. From the way the physicist stood, he had decided Westcott had passed the boundary and now existed in his own psychotically dominated personal universe.

"I don't know what's inside. But it frightens me.''

Ralston saw Westcott's IR sensor blazing its brightest red. A signal from some line-of-sight source impinged on the sensor element and caused Westcott's upset. He moved to place his gloved hand in front of the sensors. Westcott pushed him away.

"Don't. I . . . I'll lose it if you do that.''

Leonore muttered, "He's already lost it and doesn't even know it.''

Ralston looked from Westcott to the dark circle that marked the tunnel entrance. He remembered the octopus tentacle arrangement of the dome they'd found on the surface of Beta 5. There had been nothing intentionally hazardous within the dome. Their problems came from their own rush to explore rather than perverse traps set by the Betans. He saw no reason to suppose the aliens would substantially alter their planetary colonizing design on this tiny moon, even if this proved to be their main base.

"Send a probe ahead of us, fifty meters a minute max," ordered Ralston. He waited for Leonore to launch the robot sensor, then started after it. If any danger presented itself to the probe, they'd have several seconds to prepare. How, Ralston couldn't say. They carried no weapons and, he thought uneasily, no excavation equipment. If the tunnel collapsed, they'd never be able to dig out with their hands.

The four crowded close together as they made their way down the dark tunnel. Ralston switched on a headlamp and cast a sharply defined beam around the airless corridor. Westcott muttered in protest, but Ralston refused to walk in darkness, no matter how this might interfere with the mathematician's damned computer-link sensor. He thought Westcott must have picked up a com beam from an alien communication source. The IR frequency used for Westcott's computer-mind link was too useful for other purposes not to be encountered exploring an advanced culture's base.

But Ralston knew he again violated not only strict archaeological rules, but common sense as well. Having Westcott or Leonore or Bernssen remain outside to relay transmission from inside the tunnel was safe; having them pressing close, however, was comforting. Every step Ralston took, his excitement mounted. The walls nearest the dusty plain were featureless and bare. A hundred meters into the tunnel he found cryptic hieroglyphics.

Instructions? Decorations? Graffiti? Warning symbols? Ralston had no way of telling, and photographed them as he walked.

Three hundred meters brought more vivid writings on the walls, many in color and all of definite information intent.

"That one," said Bernssen. "That means don't spit on the floor."

Ralston and Leonore laughed harder than the slight joke merited, but it provided nervous release.

Ralston said, "It's more likely to tell them to slow down, that they're approaching the terminus."

"Air," muttered Westcott. "I hear it."

Leonore turned to the mathematician to tell him to be quiet, when it hit her, too. She experienced a definite pressure against the front of her suit. She said, "He's right. There's air pressure here. But where's the airlock? What holds it in?''

"I don't know," answered Bernssen, checking one of his instruments, ''but don't try breathing it. Heavy on ammonia. Enough to choke you to death in a few seconds.''

"I wasn't planning on it," said Leonore.

Ralston stopped and shined his light against the end of the tunnel. A simple sliding door ahead was all that barred them from entering the alien base. He hesitated, took a deep breath to relax, then reached out and pulled the door aside.

"An elevator?" Leonore asked, craning her neck to look around the cage. "If it is, they weren't big people. This isn't large enough for more than a dozen humans.''

"No controls," said Ralston. He kept his camera working constantly. When he got the block recorder out and ran hardcopies of the prints, he wanted to be able to study every detail of their journey.

"There are controls," said Westcott. The sensor mounted atop his head flashed once. The door closed silently, and the sudden descent caused the other three to grab one another for support. The cage stopped as abruptly as it had started, sending all four to their knees.

Ralston pulled back the simple door and shined his lamp into the corridor beyond. Dozens of tunnels radiated from it, confirming the theory that the moon had been hollowed extensively.

"Where do we start?" asked Leonore, eager now to begin.

Before Ralston could lay out a plan for exploration, Westcott walked forward, as if under intense compulsion. He went a short way down the tunnel, then turned to the left.

"Wait, dammit, don't go off like that!" shouted Ralston. The echo within his suit helmet almost deafened him. He cursed more quietly, and motioned for Bernssen and Leonore to come with him. He reset his wristcom so that they could return to this point, no matter what turnings and twistings they encountered.

But Ralston worried. The wristcom's inertial tracker worked only on a two-dimensional surface. He'd seen no reason to bring a more expensive three-dimensional unit from Novo Terra. The archaeology professor cursed the need for such cost-cutting on any expedition, and cursed Chancellor Salazar, the Alpha 3 refugees, the Betans, and his own stupidity for not planning better.

"Stop, Westcott, come back here!" he called when he reached the juncture where the mathematician had turned. Ralston shined his lamp along the corridor and saw nothing of Westcott.

"Where'd he get off to so fast?" asked Bernssen. "Do you think we're out of contact with him?"

Ralston stepped into the corridor Westcott had taken and motioned for Leonore to go back to the elevator cage. "How do you read?" he asked.

"Just fine, Michael. No signal loss."

"Come back. Westcott can hear us; he just doesn't want to admit it."

"He's acted strangely ever since we found the entrance on the surface," said Leonore. She made an ugly noise and said, "But then, he's always strange."

Ralston didn't bother pointing out that the mathematician probably overheard. He even dared to hope the insult might bring Westcott rushing back to complain. It produced no such reaction. Of the mathematician he saw no trace.

Ralston dropped to hands and knees and studied the floor.

"What're you looking for?" asked Bernssen.

"Dust. A base abandoned on a moon like this for thousands of years should be filthy with dust. There's not a speck on the floor." Ralston stood and shook his head. "I can't even find scratches showing where Westcott went by."

"Here," said Leonore, handing Ralston the four robot

probes they'd brought along. "We might as well send them out to find him. They can travel faster than Westcott, and it'll keep us from wandering around aimlessly."

Ralston silently launched the probes. They hissed in the ammonia-laced atmosphere, then vanished down the corridor the mathematician had taken. Ralston put one down each branching tunnel, until all four had left the main hallway.

"When I find him, I'm going to rip out that damned sensor by its platinum wires," Ralston grumbled. "He's going to have one chinger of a headache."

Leonore looked at her professor and shook her head. She'd seldom seen him this angry, even when he'd been dealing with Salazar and the other University bureaucrats. Ralston took off, and Leonore and Bernssen followed closely, flashing their lamps down each corridor and finding nothing but emptiness stretching as far as the headlamp's beam was capable of illuminating.

"Damn!" swore Ralston. "The probe's died on me."

"Getting some fluctuation in the ammonia level," said Bernssen, tapping the side of his analyzer. "I think it must be coming from the walls—the ammonia, I mean. Outgassing over the years."

"For ten thousand years?" Leonore sounded skeptical.

"It can happen. Especially if the atmosphere originally here had been put in under very high pressure. The porous rock walls adsorbed huge quantities, then released it slowly over the years as the pressure declined."

"I don't care about that," snapped Ralston, still angry at Westcott and his behavior. "I just want to find Westcott."

"The compression waves in the ammonia tell of something moving ahead of us," said Bernssen, growing irritated at Ralston. "It must be Westcott, verd?"

Ralston said nothing as he worked on the control for the second probe. The robot eye returned from its wanderings, hovered beside the impatient archaeologist, then took off with a faint whine to find Westcott.

"Damnation, it's gone, too," exclaimed Ralston within seconds. "What's destroying my probes?"

The words had barely left his lips when a deep virbration came up through the soles of his feet. Something ponderous and powerful operated within the corridor.

Leonore and Bernssen added the power of their headlamps to Ralston's. The three beams converged on a low-slung robot with six metallic tentacles waving in front of it. The mechanism drifted forward; due to a broad protecting skirt that brushed the floor as it moved, Ralston couldn't see if it hovered or ran on wheels. In two of the six flexing tentacles it held Ralston's robot probes, crushed and spilling their block circuits out as the robot came forward inexorably.

"I don't think it's friendly," said Bernssen, backing away. He reached out and tugged at Leonore's arm to urge her to get out of the robot's path. She tried to shake him off but the physicist was insistent. She, too, began to retreat.

"Look at the power in each of the articulated tentacle tips," muttered Ralston. "Those probes are supposed to be invulnerable to anything less than—"

"We'll sue the manufacturer," cut in Bernssen. "Let's regroup and consider what we're going to do. I don't want to end up like those probes."

Ralston hesitated. One of the tentacles took a swipe at him. The sudden electric jolt from even the close passage sent him reeling backward, arms akimbo. Leonore and Bernssen held him upright until he regained his senses.

"It looks like the night watchman," said Leonore. "I've been running my analyzer and haven't gotten any hint of motive power, age, composition, anything!"

"Wrong equipment," said Bernssen. "We aren't ready to fight it out with this one. Come on!"

Ralston disliked running from the robot, yet he saw no alternative. Westcott might be dying just on the other side of this ponderous guardian. As he edged back, Ralston cursed volubly. Nothing had gone right with this expedition. He needed time to analyze and correlate the data he gathered. Events had moved too fast for him to reflect on exactly what everything meant, where it all fit together in a grander pattern.

The Betans were the enigma that bothered him the most. The refugees from Alpha 3 had acted from necessity. Stay on their home planet and die from the random, chaotic destruction of body and culture, or else flee. Those had been their only options. Their escape had only prolonged their eventual demise.

But what of the alien Betans? Ralston hadn't a clue as to physical shape, origin, or their reason for putting an outpost on Beta 5. All he knew was what he, Leonore, and Bernssen had pieced together: the Betans probably breathed high-pressure ammonia, indicating they might be native to a gas giant. Which one? This system? Another? Was this robot slowly moving after them intentionally dangerous, or had time and the chaos device altered its programming to something less benign?

"Here, Michael. Down here," urged Leonore.

He looked and saw that the corridor she indicated narrowed substantially from the one they were in. Ralston ducked down it just a few centimeters in front of a probing robotic tentacle. The robot strained to drive its bulk after them but the rocky walls prevented it. As if caught up in a fit of human pique, the robot threw both of Ralston's probes at him. The archaeology professor easily avoided the clumsy toss.

"What now?" he asked. "We've still got to find Westcott. He might have run afoul of that automated watchdog."

"We might be able to get back into the corridor behind it, using some of the adjoining halls," said Leonore. "Send out a probe and let's see what it finds."

Ralston spent a few minutes recalling the last two probes, bringing them in high and fast over the still-raging robot guard's top. A few more minutes work had the probes exploring the depths of this auxiliary corridor.

"Its programming is obviously faulty," said Bernssen.

He frowned. "Didn't you tell me Westcott had said the Betans didn't have computers? How did they keep this monster running for so long? Or at all?"

"Westcott had only the laser disk records to work with," said Ralston. "No matter how much information he found there, he couldn't have known everything about the Betans. After all, they were obviously alien, and Westcott isn't trained to decipher hints left by alien cultures."

"Not like we are," said Leonore, with more than a hint of biting sarcasm in her voice. "Did we ever walk into this mess with our eyes wide open. We should have left someone outside to relay back—or to help us."

"The rock would have eaten our radio signals," said Bernssen.

"A fiber-optic com circuit, then," the woman said. "A few kilometers of that stuff wouldn't weigh much. We could have unrolled it as we came and—"

"There wasn't any in the supplies we brought," said Ralston, distracted. He kept track of both roaming probes and the signals they returned. What Bernssen said about absorption of signal by the rock appeared true. Less than five hundred meters dropped reception strength to a quarter of maximum.

"Who'd ever think I'd end up like this?" said Bernssen, with a small hint of humor to his words. "Mama raised me to be a physicist, and here I end up on Beta 5's moon after letting alien telepathic messages be forced onto my brain, traveling around dusty moons, being chased by a sentry robot." He shook his head in mock despair.

"That's my Nels," said Leonore. "Always looking on the bright side."

"The probe's found secondary corridors leading to Westcott," said Ralston, still worried about the weakness of his probe signals. "I'm checking to make certain one is smaller in width than our unfriendly host." He gestured obscenely in the direction of the still-straining robot. Bits of rock and dust accumulated at its base, where it ground hard against the unyielding wall.

The trio started down the corridor, and found the intersection indicated by the probe. Leonore said, "The robot's left. It must be trying to head us off."

Ralston stopped to consider their chances of returning to the main corridor and following in the robot's wake. He decided to continue along the course mapped out by his probe. Until they confronted a small guard robot, they were relatively safe.

Ralston swallowed hard when he remembered that only broad corridors led back to the elevator. If they had blundered over some activating switch and brought the robot guards to life, they'd have to run for the only way they knew back to the surface. He didn't look forward to that prospect. Ralston's arm still tingled from the electric charge the robot had given him. He wondered if the creature he'd killed with his primitive spear had felt the same before it died in its lair.

"Down there!" warned Bernssen.

To the left down a corridor meeting theirs at an acute angle, rushed the large guard robot. Ralston urged his friends on, herding them like cattle. They barely got through the intersection and into their smaller corridor when the robot began grinding against the rock and probing for them with its tentacles.

"Persistent chinger, isn't it?" said Bernssen.

"I'd like to dismantle it," said Ralston.

"We both would."

"I meant so that we could find out something about the Betans. Computer architecture can tell much about a society's thought processes. Find out what makes them design in the way they do, and you've gone a ways toward understanding them."

"All I understand is that it wants to fry my neurons," said Bernssen, in this instance not sharing Ralston's devotion to science.

Ralston stopped abruptly and pointed to a wall inset. The metal plate contained a dozen large buttons. A few of the wiggly hieroglyphs they'd noticed earlier paraded along the side of the plate; instructions for operation, Ralston guessed.

"Any idea what these do?" he asked the physicist. Bernssen shook his head. "Leonore, any ideas?"

"I don't see any of their light tubes. This segment of the tunnel doesn't appear any different from the others." Leonore shrugged. "We might press one to see."

"Too dangerous," Ralston decided. "It might call smaller guard robots."

"A fifty-fifty chance that it'd disable the big one," pointed out Bernssen.

"Too dangerous. We need a supervisor and circuit probe equipment to decipher what this controls." He glanced down at the readings from his probes. His mouth turned to cotton. Another probe had been destroyed. With only one left, they'd have to exercise even more caution—and do much of the scouting on their own.

Continuing cautiously, Ralston peered around the intersection of another large corridor with the one they traversed. He saw the battered remains of his probe on the floor. He couldn't find any trace of the cause for its destruction.

He hurried on, Leonore and Bernssen behind. As they entered the far corridor, his remaining probe gave a strong signal burst.

"Westcott!" cried Leonore. "It's found him!"

"Let's hurry. The vital signs off him don't look good. It might only be signal disruption, but I don't think so," said Ralston.

At a run, they made their way down the corridor, along a still smaller side tunnel, then into a broad corridor three times as large as the guard robot that had chased them earlier.

"No compression waves in the ammonia," announced Bernssen. "But the robot might be on idle. I can't detect that."

"The door," said Leonore, pointing. "Is Westcott behind it?"

"Definitely." Ralston saw that the door had been opened a half meter—large enough for both the mathematician and the probe to enter. "Wait here. I'll keep you posted."

"And we'll warn you if we see the robot," Leonore said anxiously. She reached out and gripped his suit sleeve. Ralston smiled weakly and patted her hand. "Be careful, Michael."

Ralston swung out into the broad expanse of the corridor and ran awkwardly for the opened door. He paused, cast his headlamp beam inside and saw nothing menacing. Here and there his bright cone of light reflected off silvered buttons and meter panels of unknown function. Not wanting to present a target for the prowling guard robot, he slipped into the room.

Ralston glanced over his shoulder and saw a familiar sight. The light switch beside the door looked identical to those in the dome on Beta 5. "I'm going to turn on the lights to get a better idea of what this room is."

"Careful," cautioned Leonore Disa.

"Here we go." He winced as he touched the switch. Only the familiar dim red lights came up. Ralston slowly turned, stopped, and shouted, "No, don't!"

But it was too late for any warning the archaeologist might give.

THIRTEEN

"DON'T, WESTCOTT, DON'T do that!" Michael Ralston shouted. The echoes inside his helmet made him instantly regret the warning. Some reactions came instinctively— even in a spacesuit. Ears ringing, he rushed forward, weight farther forward than usual in the low gravity, and grabbed for Westcott. He missed.

Westcott turned his head in such a way that the sensor unit mounted there made connection with a small red light burning on a huge instrument panel. The infrared beam from Westcott's sensor and the alien one touched, linked. The mathematician stiffened and stood with an expression of stark pain on his face.

Ralston stopped and tried to decide what to do. Through the ringing in his ears he heard Leonore's frantic voice. "Michael, what happened? Are you all right? Please answer!"

"It's Westcott. He's allowed himself to plug into the control console. At least, I think it must be the alien's central controller. It extends along an entire wall. His IR sensor locked onto the signal from an equivalent one on the panel. I don't want to break the contact because I'm not sure what it'll do to him. He said it gave him a headache when he was linked to his own computer. With this one, it might do permanent damage."

"We're coming in," came Nels Bernssen's words.

"Hurry. I need you to look over this damned panel to see if you can make anything out of it. To me it's just a hectare of meters and switches."

Ralston took Westcott's shoulders and gently shook the mathematician to see if he might get a positive response. None. The man's eyes had turned to translucent glass. His mouth hung slack and a string of drool came out one corner. All the blood had rushed from Westcott's face, giving him the look of a corpse. Ralston started to twist him around to break the IR beam when Bernssen stopped him.

"Give it a few more seconds," Bernssen said. "Can't hurt anymore, verd?"

Ralston didn't know. He might be expert at unearthing ruins thousands of years old and piecing together the day-to-day life of the former inhabitants, but in matters such as these he felt like a complete tyro. He knew enough about block computers and electronics to help him do his research and no more. There was always too much to learn, too many things to know for anyone to command it all. He had to let the physicist decide this.

"Better be quick, Nels," Leonore said. "There seems to be uncontrollable twitching in his extremities. I wonder how he can still stand."

"The beam linking him to the console," said Ralston, horror growing inside him like an ugly, crawling beast. "That's holding him in an iron grip." His concern mounted even more when he saw that Leonore's appraisal of Westcott's condition was only too accurate. The shakes spread from hands and feet through the mathematician's limbs.

"Nels, we've got to act. He's going into convulsions."

"Wait, just wait a second," the physicist said. He stood in front of the panel, hands resting on two buttons. "Here goes nothing." He leaned forward, his weight depressing both buttons.

Nothing happened.

Ralston didn't wait for Bernssen to try another possibility on the alien controller. He took Westcott by the shoulders and jerked as hard as he could. It might have been his imagination, but he thought the sensor atop Westcott's head actually tried to turn to maintain contact with the alien computer's signal. But when Westcott broke free, the muscles that had been held in rictus suddenly relaxed. The man fell in slow motion to the floor.

Ralston tried to support him and failed, forgetting that mass and inertia counted more than weight. Together, the two of them sank down in the low gravity. Ralston got to his knees and turned the mathematician onto his back. The eyes continued to stare vacantly.

"It might be bad. I get no response from his suit's life com." Just inside the faceplate of the helmet Ralston saw the vital signs readout. All stayed on neutral, as if no one wore the suit—or the occupant was dead.

"He's still breathing," said Leonore, working with Westcott's air mixture. "I've cooled off the suit by bleeding in a quick charge of oxygen. See the condensation on the inner surface of the faceplate from his breathing?"

"Still no vitals," said Ralston. He checked his remaining floater probe, silently hovering a meter away. The response from it differed from Westcott's suit reading. Definite but feeble life readings came over the broadcast circuit. "His suit might be damaged. Probably is."

Ralston turned icy at the idea that not only the suit but Westcott may have become electrically overloaded because of the connection. The man may have been rehabbed inadvertently by his reckless behavior.

"Why'd the hijo do it?" wondered Bernssen. "That's the damnedest, stupidest thing I've ever seen."

"He didn't seem to be in control. Not after we entered the complex," said Ralston. "He might have been receiving a low intensity IR input ever since we entered the exterior tunnel. Who knows how it might scramble his senses?"

Westcott's eyes focused and he began blinking and squinting, as if the dull red illumination proved too much for him. With Ralston and Leonore rubbing his arms through his suit, Westcott recovered enough to speak in a low, cracked voice.

"So vast. I . . . I was wrong. They have computers. But so strange. Not like mine. The input is wrong, so strange."

"Don't try to speak," said Ralston. "Just rest. We'll get out of here soon. You can sleep aboard the shuttle."

"I don't think so," said Bernssen. "I'm hardly an expert at what all this means, but since the only light flashing is that one—" he pointed to a dull red pulsation on the far right of the console—"and all we know for sure is that the guard robot is activated, we've got a dangerous trip ahead just reaching the surface."

"Nels, look!" Leonore took her lover's arm and moved closer.

A second light began flashing, and a third and fourth and fifth. Soon an entire army of lights glowed with an intensity matching the room's overhead illumination.

"I can't tell if Westcott activated them or this is in response to our brush with the first guardbot," said Bernssen, "but it looks as if we've got dozens of the damned things to sneak past now. I don't think we can do it. I doubt the aliens manufactured only one size of guard. Those tunnels we followed must have their own patrols by now."

"Try pressing the buttons under the lights," said Ralston. "That might turn them off."

"No!" cried Westcott. "That puts them on alert status. We'll never get free if you do that."

"You're the expert," said Bernssen, settling down on his heels near the mathematician. "What did you learn from their computer?"

"It's vast, bigger than anything I'd believed possible. But it's different, slower. As a computer it's worthless for just about every useful application." Westcott laughed harshly. "It's so slow my thought speed exceeds its cycle time."

"What caused you to go into shock?" asked Ralston.

"Its size! Never have I been inside such a large memory. I got lost. I tried to follow the usual limited pathways, but they went on to infinity. The harder I tried to return, the more confused I became. My thought speed matched the computer's, but I needed a . . . a schematic. I got lost!"

"Great," muttered Leonore. "He gets lost in the computer's memory, and we're trapped."

"Did you learn anything about the Betans? Or the condition they left this base in?" asked Ralston. "Those guard robots will kill us unless we can shut them off."

"The far side of the console, there, verd, higher, that button. Press it." Bernssen did as instructed. Westcott said, "It'll take a *wah* for them to shut down automatically."

"What?" asked Ralston.

Westcott looked sheepish. "It's a Betan time unit. I don't know how long it is. There wasn't any conversion factor, any common denominator for calculation."

"So your *wah* might last ten seconds or five thousand years?" asked Bernssen. "Still, it's better than not having the robots turned off at all. I just don't like the idea of a rescue party finding our skeletons guarded by an army of robots."

"Nels, there's not going to be any rescue party," said Leonore. "The pilot can't reach us without the shuttle." The woman clamped her jaw firmly shut and a look of pure horror crossed her face. "If we can't get back to the shuttle, the rest of the expedition on the surface of 5 is stranded! We've got the only transport up to the starship!"

"And we're pinned down for the moment," said Ralston. He took a deep breath. "The one good thing is that our suits are in full working condition." He checked his readouts. Air for another thirty hours remained. Nutrients and water in nippled tubes were close to his mouth, and the energy packs showed a virtually full charge.

"My suit's not in such good shape," said Westcott.

"Your vital signs readout? I noticed. We get a better reading off the probe," said Ralston.

"When you broke me free of the circuit," said West-cott, "all my muscles relaxed. *All* of them. The inside of my suit is quite a mess. The waste recycler came loose."

"Live with it," Bernssen said, thinking Westcott had finally received poetic justice. "It looks as if we're going to have to do something more than wait for the robots to shut down." All the indicator lights still glowed palely.

Ralston paced around the room, trying to get a feel for the architecture, the way the Betans built and thought and worked. Without any idea as to their body form, he found himself at a loss. The panels were lower than waist level, indicating they had been short. It meant nothing that there were no stools or chairs in the room. They could have been removed—or the Betans might not have used them. The controls were mostly push buttons the size of Ralston's fist. The Betans might not have good manual dexterity or, from all Ralston had seen of their robots, any digital dexterity at all. They might have been possessed of only tentacles. He finally gave up on the futile guessing game and stood next to Westcott.

"They won't come in here," said the mathematician. "The robots. This is a . . . safe area. The Betans didn't want their guards blundering about. They aren't very precisely controlled."

"Never mind that," said Ralston. "Tell us about the Betans. This base, the outpost, anything you gleaned from your connection with their computer."

Westcott frowned. "That's the odd part. I got—am still getting—this sense of dread. It has something to do with the computer. How did they keep it powered up for so many years? I got no feel for that. Only the anxiety. It might be *its* anxiety."

"That's a good point, Michael," said Bernssen. "What power source is keeping everything going? Find it, turn it off, the robots go to sleep. We don't need the lights to get out."

"If you cut all the power, though," said Leonore, "won't that kill the elevator?"

"She's right," said Ralston. "We're better off doing as little as possible since we don't know what we are doing. We're trapped for the moment. Until that off-switch returns them to standby."

"In a damned *wah*, whatever that is," grumbled Bernssen. The physicist began studying the console with as much success as Ralston had achieved deciding on the Betans' body size and shape.

"This entire complex, the computer, everything," said Westcott, "is a prototype. That I did learn for certain. None of this had ever been done before."

"This and the outpost on 5 were their first?" Leonore let out a low whistle. "I'm impressed. As impressed as I am with Dial and the other refugees from Alpha 3. Did necessity push the Betans? Did they know of the chaos device and try to escape it, too?"

"They knew," said Westcott. "There's so much stored within the computer. It's so huge."

"I know, you got lost," Ralston said impatiently. "What of the Betans? Their detection of the chaos device? Did you happen to get a hint of what they looked like?"

"Or how to operate this console," cut in Nels Bernssen. "There doesn't seem to be any simple order to it." Bernssen dropped flat onto his back and kicked under the console to begin tracing wiring. Ralston considered this a fruitless pursuit, but it kept the physicist busy. And Ralston would be the first to admit that any information would aid them. Any at all.

Westcott moved closer to the panel, his face haunted. "It's so hard for me to keep from reestablishing a linkup. Keep me away. It frightens me."

"But it also intrigues you, doesn't it?" asked Leonore. "You're afraid, but you're also afraid you'll miss something important."

"It's all in there. I know it. But it'd take so long to find it. And the entire computer's a prototype, too. Just like the rest of the base.''

Ralston went to the console and gripped the IR sensor there. With a mighty jerk, he broke it free and turned the sensing element toward the wall, where it wouldn't interfere with Westcott.

''Thank you,'' the mathematician said, sounding sincere. ''It truly draws me, just like a Siren's call.''

The classical allusion startled Ralston. He hadn't thought Westcott read anything but mathematical treatises, then realized the man had access to everything within a computer, not just its computational capabilities. Some of the other stored bytes must have registered on his wired brain as he haunted the circuits of the University computer.

''Now, Dr. Westcott,'' said Leonore, settling onto the floor next to the mathematician, ''we need to know what you discovered. If you don't begin soon, we might have to turn that sensor back around and do some checking on our own.''

Ralston started to protest his assistant's behavior. He checked his outburst. Westcott was uncooperative at the best of times—and these were far from that. If Leonore's thinly veiled threat produced results, he wasn't going to say a word.

Westcott began babbling to the point that Leonore had to stop him several times and gently calm him.

''The Betans,'' she prompted. ''What of them?''

''They came from this system. Beta 7. It's a gas giant. They breathe a standard CH_4 and NH_3 mixture under high pressure. You already know that. There was something different about the leader of the expedition that established this base and the outpost on Beta 5.''

''Different in what way?'' asked Ralston, finding himself engrossed more and more in Westcott's telling. He checked twice to be certain his recorder caught every syllable of the descriptions.

''Unusual, different, psychotic. He wasn't like the rest of them. I can't say how. There's so much lost in the depths of that computer. It's so huge! Not even the University computer has—"

"The Betans," urged Leonore.

"Yes, yes," Westcott said irritably. "There's another base similar to this one on the outermost moon circling Beta 7. It was from there that—they don't seem to have names—the one who established this base made the observations of the chaos field as it entered the system."

"How close did it pass the primary?" asked Bernssen, still buried under the control console. "Within a dozen A.U.'s?"

"Less than an eleventh of an A.U. The . . . observer noted it pass through the photosphere. I have no idea what equipment he used to record it, if he even did. There is a lack of curiosity about the universe that borders on the obscene."

"Are those laser disks likely to hold the information about the chaos device?" asked Ralston.

"Not the ones you gave me. I've already told you about them. But there might be more on the Beta 7 moon. Not here. This base was stripped of all but the heaviest equipment when the chaos effects began manifesting themselves."

"What happened to the Betan?"

"He wasn't affected, but the equipment began malfunctioning. The computer shows signs of failure throughout due to the chaos field's effects. The solution to the chaos equations lies within this machine. I know it."

"The other moon. The one circling Beta 7. Would it have a better functioning computer? One you might get better information from?" Ralston began worrying about this expedition.

The chaos effects closed in around them. Ralston closed his eyes and tried not to worry. The sun prepared itself for explosion, the animals on Beta 5 exhibited nonviable mutations that had to be a result of a continuing chaotic influence, the Alphan dioramas had induced an epileptic fit in him—but both Bernssen and Leonore escaped through proper medication—the alien base had been abandoned, all because of the roving chaos field.

The chaos field.

Ralston itched inside over that unseen alien enigma. Who had created it? Why did it exist? It both gave him the opportunity of a lifetime and robbed him of those same fabulous archaeological sites. He had to know.

And the answer lay on a distant moon.

Before Ralston could ask Westcott any further questions, Leonore said, "The lights! They're going out. Does that mean the robots are turned off?"

Bernssen scooted from under the console. "I think it does. I traced some of the circuits to a single black box. When the lights started going out, I felt the box vibrate as if mechanical relays were closing. I'll give the Betans one thing—they knew how to build to last. It doesn't seem that this place is a prototype. They did some good work." He shook his head at Westcott's contention that this was the first—and possibly the only—base ever built.

Ralston peered out the door and cast his lamp beam down the broad corridor. He saw nothing.

"Do you think it's really safe?" asked Leonore. Her eyes never strayed from the indicator lights, as if she expected them to flash on again in mockery of her hope.

"It looks like the best chance we've had," said Ralston. "I'll send the probe out to backtrack our course here."

"No," said Westcott, his voice almost breaking with strain. "Map out and scout the most direct route to the elevator. I don't want to stay here any longer than I must."

Ralston silently sent the probe flashing into the darkness. He adjusted his controls, made a few corrections to peak the signal, and waited. For long minutes the probe floated through the long corridors. Twice it noted inert robots. Then came the slow flash of a green lamp on Ralston's control unit.

"It's waiting for us at the elevator," Ralston said. He heard three sets of lungs release pent-up breath.

While the probe had cleared the path, Ralston still proceeded cautiously. They passed the silent guard robots, their tentacles dangling loosely at their sides. No other evidence of habitation presented itself to them before they, too, stood in front of the elevator door.

"I'm glad, now, that we didn't try to kill all the power," said Leonore. "Passing through here is scary enough. To be trapped here . . ."

They entered the elevator. As the door closed, Ralston couldn't help taking a quick peek around the edge and giving a slight shudder. He had violated every tenet of good xenoarchaeology and had lived to tell about it. He almost came to believe in luck. Almost.

"This chaos thing you're always talking about—that's what's scrambled your brains, isn't it?" The pilot floated a meter away, arms crossed, legs twined together in a knot that belied bones. His expression matched his tone.

"We need to go to Beta 7," insisted Ralston. "Can the shuttle make it?"

"Impossible. Unless you want to strand those men on 5. Go on, do that. See if they won't complain."

"Not enough fuel left," Bernssen said, all energy gone from his voice. "That's the problem. We need what fuel's left to land the shuttle and retrieve the expedition."

"One trip for the men, two for men and equipment," said the pilot. "And that's depending on everything going without a problem. The way you people operate, I wouldn't count on anything happening the way you planned."

Ralston ignored the sarcasm. The pilot had every right to be upset with them. They had exited the Betan base on the outer moon and immediately signaled for rendezvous. The pilot had expertly matched with them on his first figure-eight orbit around Beta 5 and the moon, then began shouting that he should have abandoned them when Ralston told of their need to go to the gas giant.

The pilot had done more than required every time they'd

asked. To take such a foolish risk now violated the pilot's code, not to mention going past the bounds of rationality.

"Can't you get us a low energy Hohmann orbit?" asked Bernssen.

"Sure, punch it up yourselves. Take a look at it."

"No need," said Westcott, eyes slightly glassy and his mouth slack. The sensor atop his freshly shaved head blinked balefully. "We'd be eleven months to arrive, and a seven-month stay allows us a fourteen-month return."

"That's almost three years!" blurted Leonore Disa. "We might not have that long. The sun's going nova in a year or two."

"We don't have the supplies, either," pointed out Ralston. "We need to blast directly."

"Can't be done. No fuel. Figures don't lie. Ask that one, the freak computer man with the hardware head." The pilot lifted his chin in Westcott's direction.

"What if we didn't take the shuttle," said Ralston, thinking out loud. "If we used the starship, we could—"

"*No!*" The pilot's denial was both immediate and emphatic. "That's dangerous!"

"The stardrive interaction with gravity wells around planets is unpredictable," said Westcott. "An interesting effect in the theory I'm working on."

"The chaos equations?" asked Ralston, confused.

"Before that, before you brought such a fine problem to my attention, I spent my time deriving a new quantum gravity theory. Very difficult geometry involved."

They each floated in midair, surrounded by a tiny shell of silence in the central chamber's low atmospheric pressure. Ralston's mind worked over their dilemma. The shuttle was out of the question; only the starship could be used, but that posed problems of a nature they wouldn't be able to overcome.

"We might be getting ahead of ourselves on this," said Ralston. "The Betans might not have survived. We're talking about their abandonment of this base almost ten thousand years ago. Westcott wasn't sure about their motives in founding the outpost. They might have been refugees from cataclysm on their planet.''

"Odd choice, isn't it?'' asked Leonore. "If they're native to a gas giant, why would they flee to a stony planet? There's another gas giant in the system almost identical to 7.''

"What I'm saying is that we don't know if there's anything to find on Beta 7. Let's rig a probe and send it. If it finds evidence of the Betans, we can return to the problem of reaching them. If it doesn't, we've saved ourselves a lot of work.''

"A probe we can arrange,'' grumbled the pilot. "Too bad you all can't be stuffed into it.'' He expertly rolled in midair, caught an elastic strap, and levered himself across the room, hitting the shaft leading to the cockpit with contemptuous ease.

"It's off,'' said Leonore, watching the radar screen. A tiny green dot crept away from them, looping once around Beta 5 to pick up speed and then be slung from the gravity well on its way to Beta 7.

"With constant acceleration we won't have long to wait. By the end of the week we'll check it for midcourse corrections,'' said Bernssen. "In two we'll be nearing 7.''

"Any idea about a radiation field around the destination?'' asked Ralston. "I don't want the instrumentation fried. That won't tell us anything.''

"We're taking a chance, as is,'' said Bernssen. "I've got the probe protected, more against solar flares than planetary radiation belts, but it'll be verd all the way.''

Ralston still worried for the entire three weeks until it arrived in orbit around Beta 7.

Then they all started worrying in earnest. The probe found definite indications of life on the surface of the gas giant. The race that had built the outposts on Beta 5 and its moon still lived—and might still have detailed knowledge of the chaos device and its passage through their solar system.

FOURTEEN

"THE SIGNALS COME back too slowly," complained Michael Ralston. He spun slowly in the starship's passenger compartment, irritated at the need to be inactive.

"The speed of light is the best I can do," said Bernssen. Turning to Leonore Disa, the physicist said jokingly, "You ought to find an alien dig with ftl communication gear for your professor. That'd get you a degree in nothing flat."

"If I ever found anything like that," Leonore said, "I'd go into business for myself and put Daddy and IC out of business." She chuckled, adding, "That'd drive him *crazy!*"

"The signal quality isn't very good, either. Can't you boost the gain?" Ralston found himself becoming as singleminded as Westcott about this project. The data from the surface of Beta 5 continued to come in as the ultrasonic digger continued its work on the Alphan refugees' city, but nothing as exciting as the information gathered by Bernssen and Leonore—and himself—from the diorama.

He shook his head as he thought about those messages. How far he'd come since blundering into the diorama and experiencing the Alphans' warning to generations then unborn. He'd discovered Fennalt's attempt to create a new city out of the Betans' abandoned outpost and the intricate maze of tunnels in the hollowed-out moon, with its still functional equipment, and now he had found a living alien race on Beta 7's ammonia-cloaked surface.

And Ralston hated it. He hadn't followed correct procedures at any stage. He had lost valuable information. He knew he missed a great deal, lost it for all time due to the pressures of exploration. He felt more like Bishop de Landa destroying the Mayan codices than he did a preserver of ancient lore.

Ralston almost cried, thinking of their blundering through the moon's tunnels. Activating guard robots alone had been a major sin for any archaeologist, but he had allowed Westcott to tap into the Betans' computer without the necessary months of study and discussion of precautions. He could have restrained the mathematician, kept him from wandering off once they had entered the elevator. He should have realized the danger in exploring the alien base. Ralston had only himself to blame, yet if Westcott hadn't resurrected the long-slumbering computer memory, they wouldn't have known about the Betans' existence on the gas giant.

"It's all going too fast for me to analyze," he said. "I feel as if I'd been run back in time to the Nex-P'torra war. There was never time to relax and reflect then. Always, we dashed from star to star, fought on one planet after another, then hurried on until I didn't know or care where we were." He looked at Leonore, who nodded slowly. "I feel that way now," Ralston said.

"I understand," said Leonore. "Any of the sites we've found deserve major funding and intensive work—years of work. We've skimmed the top, and possibly done more harm than good."

"That probe circling Beta 7 will be the determination of whether we succeed or fail miserably," said Ralston. "The Betans might not know their star is pre-nova. We can warn them, though what good that'll do, I can't say. If Nels is right, they'd have only a handful of years to build ships and escape."

"You don't think the government would be willing to send rescue ships for them?" asked Bernssen.

"For ammonia and methane breathers used to living beneath a kilobar of atmosphere? The Church would raise the issue of whether they possessed a soul and cloud the issue. By the time any of the bureaucrats could see how a rescue would benefit their careers, the Beta primary would have exploded."

"Don't sound so bitter, Michael," chided Leonore. "There are others who might help in a rescue mission."

"The P'torra? Hardly. The Nex were too devastated by the war to do more than hold their own boundaries. None of the other races I can think of have any major starfaring capability."

"It hardly seems moral for us to interrogate them for information on the chaos field and then let them die from its effects," said Bernssen. 'But what other choice do we have?"

"I can't see any," Ralston said bleakly.

"You, back there," came the pilot's annoyed voice over the intercom. "New signals from your probe. Check them and clear the channel. I need to talk to the poor chingers you left on the ground. We're overdue for their progress reports."

Bernssen twisted around and went to his makeshift control panel. He worked for a few minutes, then frowned.

"What's wrong, Nels?" asked Leonore.

"I didn't collect the entire message. Wait a second and let me decode."

The physicist started clumsy console work. Westcott pushed him aside. Bernssen started to react angrily, then subsided and let the mathematician direct-connect to the computer. In seconds, Westcott's face turned flaccid, all humanity gone. When he blinked and turned from the console, he smirked.

"You have no luck whatsoever," he said. "The probe reports a retrograde satellite, the one farthest out."

"What of it?" demanded Ralston, anxious to cut through Westcott's gloating.

"It's outfitted similar to the one around 5. Hollow, heavily instrumented, abandoned." Westcott's smirk grew into a grin that split his face. "Then the probe died."

"Died?" Ralston echoed.

"No more. *Pop!*" Westcott made a small exploding gesture with his hands.

"There goes any chance of contacting the Betans," said Bernssen. "A constant monitoring of the usual radio frequencies hasn't turned up which they use, if any."

"They might not radiate," said Leonore. "Look at Earth's com development. It took less than a hundred years to use microburst pulses relayed through communication satellites. And fiber optics were very common for ground communication. Almost no leakage to space with either of those technologies."

"The probe didn't find any artificial satellites," said Bernssen. "But that doesn't mean anything. It made fewer than a dozen orbits before it died."

"No chance of reviving it? A chance burst of radiation might have blanked out the rest of the signal," suggested Ralston.

Westcott shook his head and smiled until the corners of his mouth must have hurt from the strain. "The probe failed permanently and irretrievably," the mathematician said smugly. "You neglected to plan for all possible contingencies."

"Go plug yourself back into the Betans' computer and see if I care," snapped Ralston. He shoved himself away from the control console and came to rest at the far side of the compartment. Leonore drifted over to join him.

"Michael, don't let him upset you. He's not human. He spends all his time with computers. This might be Westcott's first real contact with others in years."

"He doesn't teach that many classes at the University," Ralston conceded. "But there's no reason for such childish behavior. He *delights* in my failure!"

"Westcott may not know any better." She glanced over her shoulder at Westcott and Bernssen, who still argued. "He may never learn, either. But we can use him."

"What? How?"

"I've been discussing this with the pilot. If Westcott hooked directly into the starship's computer and controlled a shift, we might be able to hop out to Beta 7. Nels and I discussed it, we've talked with the pilot and with the others down below at Nels' observatory, and there's no other chance."

"Why can Westcott do something the on-board computer can't?"

"The programming. The pilot is good but Westcott is better. He knows the computer intimately in ways no one unlinked can. For such a precise shift, Westcott is perfect. His field of expertise is quantum gravity theory. He said so. Remember? He can negotiate the gravity wells and calculate well enough to drop us within a thousand kilometers of the satellite the probe found."

"And then we could examine *that* outpost and maybe contact the Betans directly," Ralston said, his enthusiasm for the attempt waxing. "They must have left some equipment linking the outpost with their surface launch site."

"There's no way we could ever land on the surface of Beta 7," pointed out Leonore. "This is a chance to warn them, if they don't already know of the nova, and also to find out what they learned about the chaos field. You know what I think? I think that the chaos field might be what drove them off Beta 5. If it is, they have detailed observations. Nels needs that; so do we."

"Will Westcott do it?" asked Ralston.

"He'll do it," the woman solemnly assured him. "Or I'll promise him a long walk home."

For a split second, Ralston wasn't certain which he'd rather see. Then scientific necessity reasserted itself over personal antipathy. They were starring to Beta 7!

· · ·

"I don't like it. Not at all. You chingers haven't shown yourselves to be any good at this. Damn! Wish I'd drawn Velasquez and that Proteus assignment. But no, I get . . ."

The pilot's acid words trailed off as Westcott positioned himself before the ship's main control panel. The small sensor recently installed on the console flashed its baleful infrared message. Westcott tipped his head forward until his sensor locked with the output beam. The mathematician's body went rigid.

"I'll never get over seeing him like that," said Ralston.

"You'll never get used to it if the chinger wrecks us," warned the pilot. As caustic as the man sounded, he was drawn to the ease with which Westcott worked in conjunction with the computer's intricate starfaring programs. Lights flashed and indicators began giving readings in agreement with the pilot's laboriously planned shift. "Damn, but he controls the ship better than I could."

Ralston could never find it in his heart to envy Westcott. Pitying the mathematician took all his surplus emotion.

"Here we goooo!" cried the pilot.

Acceleration slammed them back into their couches. As abruptly as it had come, the invisible hand changed position and pushed forward against the restraining webs.

"Exact position to the tenth decimal place," the pilot said, awe tinging his voice. "Damn, but I wish I could do that." He eyed Westcott's sensor, then shook his head.

"I've got the probe on visual," came Bernssen's excited voice. The vidscreen flickered, then formed into the image of Ralston's twisted and broken probe, its electronic guts spilled onto the dusty plain of the retrograde moon.

"No sign of weaponry," Ralston muttered, more to himself than to the others. "What brought it down like that?"

"Chaos," came Westcott's reply.

Ralston spun and almost collided with the mathematician. "Any sign of life on the moon?" he asked, to cover his surprise at Westcott's nearness. He had been so engrossed in the problem, he'd ignored everything around him.

"None. The pilot says we can descend using the shuttle. There will be very little fuel usage."

"Can we make more than one trip?" asked Leonore, obviously interested in exploring, then doing real archaeology.

"One trip only," said Westcott. "The fuel is at a lower limit now for a one-shot safe retrieval of those back on 5."

Ralston motioned for them to get into their suits. He wanted to get started as soon as possible.

'I protest!" Leonore Disa shouted. "You can't do this!"

"Explain it to her, Nels," Ralston said.

"*Madre de Dios*, you do it," said the physicist, fastening the last strap of his suit.

"I want to go. You can't keep me back." Leonore floated with arms crossed just a few centimeters away.

"Fuel limitations," said Ralston. "One less to go, less mass to boost back, even against four-percent gravity. Bernssen is needed to study the equipment, Westcott is willing to connect to any computer we find, and I'm in charge." Ralston took a deep breath. "We violated every law of xenoarchaeology and good sense before. Not this time. You'll stay aloft with the starship and monitor our every communication."

"Which will be nil when you go into the tunnels to get to the Betans' computers," raged Leonore.

"This time, we're setting up a com-link to relay out our signal," said Bernssen.

"You just don't want me to go because you think it's dangerous. You can't do this, Michael. And you, Nels. You're not even arguing with him!"

"It *is* dangerous," said Ralston. "And there's no one else I'd rather have along than you. We've been through too much for me to not know your abilities, Leonore. This is a pragmatic decision." He smiled slowly. "Only one archaeologist is needed. And you don't expect *me* to stay behind, do you?''

"Yes," she said, not meaning it. Her anger faded. "You'd better bring back everything we need, Dr. Ralston. If you don't, I'll go fetch it myself!''

"Agreed." Ralston buttoned up the last fasteners on his suit and made sure that both Westcott and Bernssen checked his seals; he did the same for them. Even triple-checking sometimes afforded room for mistakes. On this quick in-and-out expedition there could be no mistakes at all. Ralston knew they'd been inordinately lucky before. A second time they couldn't count on luck.

They slipped into the shuttle, with Bernssen again at the controls. The pilot had programmed exactly, and the physicist's minimal skills weren't required. Ralston heaved a sigh of relief when the rockets died under them. As before, the vidscreens showed immense clouds of soft dust billowing around. This moon was half the size of the other they'd explored; the major difference, as Ralston saw it, was the presence of Beta 7 in the sky. The giant filled the sky with an awesome sight of colorful gas bands and raging storms.

Ralston shook himself from the view. He was no mere tourist. He had left Leonore behind to lead this expedition—and with leadership came worry. He swallowed harder, thinking that anything might happen to Westcott. Without the mathematician's direct-link to the ship's computer, shifting back to the inner planet would be difficult for the pilot.

Without the shuttle, it might not matter. The pilot wouldn't be able to pick up the scientists still on 5's surface doing their astronomical observations.

"Got the equipment?" asked Bernssen, settling his own load. They had scavenged much from ship's stores. In addition to the transmitter relays they'd place every time they turned a corner within the tunnel system they expected to find, Ralston had pulled free almost a kilometer of fiber optic from the starship's guts. With a small crawler robot and a dust-grain camera, he hoped to bypass the guard robots and not awaken them from their centuries of downtime.

"All set," said Ralston. He cast a quick glance at Westcott, who weaved off-balance under his load, in spite of the low gravity. Together they left the shuttle and started across the dusty plain for an infrared source they'd detected from orbit.

"That's it," said Bernssen with some satisfaction. "I didn't think anything natural would have a thermal portrait like that." The tunnel mouth had been hewn in a perfectly circular pattern.

Reaching it, Ralston dropped the most powerful of the transmitter relays. "Leonore, you read?"

"Reading verd," came her immediate answer. "We're almost directly overhead."

Ralston craned his neck and saw a bright spot moving across the airless sky. Behind loomed Beta 7, majestic behind its cloak of swirling gases and typical Jupiter storms. His muscles began to knot. Ralston turned back to the job, setting the microburst relay. Every time the transmitter received a signal from Leonore in the starship, it would spew forth the entire conversation recorded since the last pulse. With the triggering signal, Leonore could send any information she thought they'd need.

"Start the crawler," Ralston told Westcott, "while I finish with this."

The mathematician pulled out a robot hardly larger than his hand. Tracks ran on either side, and a large spiked wheel could be lowered for terrain requiring more traction than that afforded by the treads. Westcott attached the miniature camera, its optics system no larger than a dust mote. Bernssen set up a reel with the fiber-optic cable and attached one end to the crawler and the dust-grain camera. The other end he fixed to the transmitter.

"Good visual," came Leonore's acknowledgment. "Good hunting. Damn you all!"

Ralston waited nervously as the crawler started off on its

slow exploration of the entry tunnel, down a spiraling ramp, and through a variety of rooms. Twice it passed an inert guard robot without activating it.

"Good choice of equipment," said Westcott, with unexpected praise. "Finding a ramp was lucky, too. Saves losing the fiber in a closing door." The mathematician beamed unexpectedly. "I have a good idea how to reach the main computer console. An analysis of the geometry used in designing the tunnels shows a central hub—turn left! Yes, down that direction." Westcott stood and peered at the tiny monitor screen.

Ralston guided the crawler in the direction indicated. After less than a hundred meters he saw a door similar to the one on the moon half a solar system away.

"How do we get there?" asked Bernssen. "The crawler went by a pair of the robots. We'd activate them."

"Use the wheel to enter the room," said Westcott. Ralston sweated freely by the time he lowered the large geared wheel and worked open the control-room door. Inside he sent the crawler directly for the right side of the console. The faint IR imaging failed to pick up the buttons that disabled the robots.

Westcott took over. How he managed to become so adroit using remotes, Ralston could only guess. Perhaps the mathematician considered this a primitive extension of his linkup with a computer. Maybe he'd practiced for some other chore at some other time. Ralston cared only that Westcott got the crawler onto the control console and ran the spiked wheel over the appropriate large control buttons.

"What do we do, wait a *wah* for them to turn off?" asked Bernssen.

"They were never activated. This ensures they won't come on," said Westcott. "And I timed the *wah* duration to be four seconds longer than four minutes."

"Maybe they'll rename it after you," Bernssen said sarcastically.

Bernssen hefted a pack and started into the tunnel,

Ralston and Westcott following. At every turn they dropped a relay transmitter and checked its operation. Ralston wanted their every move recorded.

He jumped when Leonore's voice boomed in his helmet, "How's it going?"

"No problems yet," he answered. "Have you orbited once already?"

"Verd. The pilot doesn't want to change altitude. Once around every sixty-one minutes."

"I'm putting the crawler on random walk through the tunnels to record as much as possible before we have to leave."

"The pilot wanted me to tell you to bring back as much of the fiber optic as possible. He doesn't like not being in contact with all the hull sensors."

"Verd."

Ralston and the others stopped just short of the first guard robot. The archaeologist pointed to his helmet. They pressed their helmets together and shouted at one another to keep from broadcasting on a band that would arouse the guard.

"How sure are you that the robot is disabled?" he shouted at Westcott.

The mathematician, looking irritated that Ralston challenged his judgment in such matters, swung off past the robot guard without hesitation. As if he walked on ice, Ralston slipped past the robot, sure that it would blink once and start reaching for him with its electrified tentacles.

Nothing of the sort happened. They passed the second robot, and only then did Ralston start to breathe more easily. By the time they'd entered the control room, Ralston's apprehension had turned once more to excitement. He was a field xenoarchaeologist with an entire site to explore!

"Don't touch those buttons," Ralston warned Bernssen, as the physicist started toward the controls for the robots. "I don't want to fight my way out this time."

"With what? Your bare hands? We don't have any more weapons now than we did before." Bernssen snorted and dived under the control console to begin mapping out the circuits in an effort to determine how the Betans controlled their equipment.

Ralston touched a bulge in his pack. He hadn't told the others, but he had spent the better part of four hours assembling a laser capable of burning through a robot's metallic body. It had been several years since he'd fought beside the Nex, but their training had stayed with him. Given time, Ralston felt confident he could assemble a device capable of destroying the entire complex.

But destruction wasn't what brought him here. He needed data. On the Betans. On their artifacts. On the chaos device.

"I'm recalling the crawler to make a more systematic search," he told the others. Bernssen grunted acknowledgement; Westcott simply stood and stared at the console. Ralston had the image of a high diver in mind. Westcott looked as if he summoned the courage to make the first step that would send him plummeting toward a distant patch of water.

The crawler returned and Ralston sent it back along a nearby corridor. As it rolled, he stayed well back and photographed every room he came to. Once, the crawler detected a robot sentry; Ralston backed up the tiny probe and the camera it carried and sent them exploring down another tunnel.

One room in particular fascinated him. Nowhere in the complex weavings of tunnels had he seen anything he'd label as art. In this small rock-walled room he found paints squirted across the walls in patterns he took to be representational.

"I'm getting a good photo," came Leonore's voice. Again Ralston jumped. He hadn't realized they'd been in the base this long. "Are they decent depictions?" she asked.

"Who can say without actually meeting one of the Betans?" he answered. "There's something peculiar about this room, other than the art. It seems familiar, like I've been here, but I know that's not possible.''

Ralston hesitated, thinking hard. Instinct often gave him a better idea than rigidly following procedures outlined by scholars a hundred light years distant.

''What's wrong, Michael?'' Leonore sounded worried.

''Nothing. Nothing's wrong. I have the oddest feeling of having entered one of the Alphan dioramas. I don't feel the beginning of the telepathic projection, though.'' Ralston bent forward and examined one wall. What he'd first thought to be part of the picture turned out to be a smaller metallic panel with two large buttons. Designs had been scrawled across the surfaces, making them blend into those on the wall.

''Don't press it. Get Nels. Let him examine it.''

''I'm not touching it, Leonore,'' he said. Dropping to his knees, Ralston shone his headlamp directly onto the buttons. Of the circuits behind, he saw nothing. ''This is frustrating. Maybe it only activates some art display.''

''Michael,'' she warned.

Caution forgotten, Ralston brushed across the righthand button. Pale light came up in the room and the images began to flow sluggishly. He rocked back and simply stared in fascination as the blurred images began to take on more distinct form.

''It's like an ancient moving picture,'' he said. ''I wonder if it's telling a story? Without a slight ammonia atmosphere in here, I can't pick up any vibrations. I'd think any high pressure being would be especially sensitive to sound.''

''You shouldn't have done that, Michael,'' Leonore scolded. ''Nels is on his way. Westcott, too.''

''No need. I haven't done anything.'' Ralston got no reply. He guessed that the starship had passed beyond line-of-sight with the transmitter again. All he said would be recorded for the next flyover burst transmission.

The figures continued to move, but were still vague. ''I think these may be exact replicas of the Betans. They have no rigid shape, but flow amorphously, like a jellyfish. I have no idea what the red currents that seem to flow in and out of the creatures represents. Nutrients? Exhaust heat?''

"Michael, there you are!" Bernssen almost collided with the rock wall, misjudging the low gravity in his haste. "How'd you find this place?"

"Just happened across it. It must be a vidscreen for tri-dee programming, though it is primitive."

"It's the communication center."

"What do you mean?" Ralston stared at the physicist.

"Westcott tapped into the computer once more. I gave him a one-minute jaunt, then blanked his sensor. Together with the way the leads from the console ran in this direction, we decided this is what we've been looking for."

"This is a com center? Ridiculous. Those are . . . real?"

Westcott came to stand near the dual button controls. "As close as we can determine, this is a live picture beamed up from the surface of Beta 7."

"What's the other button do?"

"Try it," urged Bernssen. "Westcott hit a dead end trying to find information on the chaos field."

"The history left in their computer memory only confused me," the mathematician said. "Dr. Bernssen and I mutually discovered that this studio existed."

"A broadcast studio," murmured Ralston. He shook his head in disbelief.

Westcott reached past and touched the left-hand button. For several minutes, nothing seemed to happen. Then Ralston tried to cover his ears. The sudden ear-splitting roar coming through the suit speakers rivaled a rocket blast.

Westcott twitched uncomfortably and touched the button again. By this time Bernssen had removed the metallic panel, to expose a wrist-thick band of wires. He took a sensor similar to the one Westcott had mounted on his skull and placed it near the bundle.

"Which ones?" Bernssen asked the mathematician, with

some distaste. Westcott pointed, and Bernssen severed the wires and placed the sensor into the circuit.

"What are you doing?"

"Linking to the computer again," said Westcott. He turned his head so that the IR beams intersected. His body stiffened but he forced himself to keep talking. "I now have a linkup that allows communication. How well this works is unknown."

"Put out a general call," urged Ralston. He crowded close and stared at the images flowing around the room. One of the images stopped and seemed to peer in. "There, direct your request to that one."

"I . . . I have. He-she-it is not interested." Even as Westcott spoke, the creature faded away. "Their life is unusual. There is no . . . threat."

"The chaos field. Tell them about the danger from the chaos field!" cried Ralston, agitated now. He refused to allow such an opportunity to slip past him.

"They do not care. They have no predators on Beta 7."

"That's not possible," said Bernssen. "Where's the goad to advance?"

"They absorb nutrients from the atmosphere. Not osmosis. A different process. But how?" Westcott's voice rose to a wail. "Curiosity. An aberration. Not allowed, scorned by truly civilized beings. Why have we come?"

Ralston jerked around and saw another fuzzy shape peering in, as if they were specimens in a cage. His eyes darted to the open doorway before returning to the creature who somehow addressed them through Westcott's mind-computer linkage.

"Why are you here?" repeated Westcott, his voice cracking under the strain of input from the alien computer.

"We seek information, to give you information," said Ralston, trying to keep calm. Few of even the most successful scouts ever discovered another life form. One in a million found intelligent life.

"Why? That is sick. They all tell me this is so."

"Give information on this outpost," requested West-cott. "And the one on Beta 5's moon."

"Those? I built them. I am sick and unwanted by others."

"You?" asked Ralston. "Ask it to explain, Westcott. Ask it!"

The creature flowed and changed shape as an unseen and unfelt breeze gusted past. "I left the surface of this planet many rotations ago because I am unwell in my thoughts and pursuits. Passage of a peculiar cometary object unreasonably excited me."

"The chaos device?" Ralston asked.

"The peculiar cometary object," the gaseous creature went on, using Westcott as its voice, "displayed none of the attributes I had calculated. We do much of a theoretical nature, little of a substantive. Except for I, who am forever sick."

"The cometary object," said Ralston. "Tell us about it."

"I have that data," cut in Westcott, his voice lower. Tears ran down the mathematician's cheeks. "The strain of maintaining this contact is too much for me. I can't keep it much longer."

Ralston found himself caught between his desire to learn as much about the Betans as possible and the need to warn them of the impending solar explosion.

"Tell him about the nova and how it was caused by the chaos device—what he calls the cometary object."

"Verd, but it'll be the last I can send," said Westcott, his entire body trembling with exertion.

Ralston slipped closer and peered into the mathematician's helmet to read the vital signs. For once, Westcott wasn't acting willfully. His blood pressure was at a dangerous level, and blood electrolytes had fallen mysteriously to a danger point.

"Warn them," urged Ralston.

Westcott gasped and fell forward, breaking the sensors' IR beam. Ralston cradled the quaking man in his arms.

The gas creature to whom they'd spoken shifted and moved away, becoming increasingly blurred as it left.

"Did you warn them?" asked Bernssen, helping Ralston support Westcott.

"I did. He . . . he said I was sick, too. They have no fear of death, no reason to live except that is what they've always done. He wasn't even interested!"

"We're leaving," said Ralston. "Now. We're getting Westcott back to the starship. He's been through enough."

But as Ralston left the communication room, a pang of guilt assailed him. He knew they did the proper thing in returning Westcott to the medical facilities aboard the ship, but now he wanted to explore just a little longer!

FIFTEEN

"HE'S RESTING COMFORTABLY," said Leonore Disa, "but the pilot is threatening to toss him out the airlock." She settled into a half huddle in midair, one leg hooked around an elastic cord. "Frankly, I'm inclined to help the pilot."

Ralston inwardly groaned. Ever since leaving the treasure trove on Beta 7's moon, Westcott had caused nothing but trouble. He hadn't wanted to be treated by the ship's automedic. When they forced him, he didn't want the injections prescribed. By then the automed had already performed its duty. Westcott fought the administered sedative to the point of hooking himself into the ship's computer and ordering a stimulant. Only the pilot's quick thinking had prevented the automed from obeying the larger computer's command.

"What's he doing now?" Ralston asked, not wanting to know.

"He insists that he must work on the data accumulated. He refuses to do anything else, even eat. The man's gaunt to the point of starvation when he's in his usual condition. Now?" Leonore shook her head. "I don't understand how sheer stubbornness can keep him going. But it is, verd, it is!"

"What data did he get?" asked Bernssen. "I didn't

185

think he got anything significant from the Betan he contacted.''

"I didn't, either," said Ralston, curious. "We need Westcott in top shape to shift back to Beta 5. Let me go talk to him.''

"Take a wrench with you," called Leonore. "You'll need to bash him over the head a few times just to get his attention." Disgusted, she drifted away, to where she and Nels Bernssen could talk in private.

Ralston hurried along the central shaft of the starship and found the medical cabin. Inside, the distinction between walls and ceiling proved even more elusive than in other portions of the ship. Equipment sprang from every available flat surface. In the center of what appeared to be a clumsy spider's web, hung the mathematician.

Westcott grumbled constantly and tried to reach the sensor mounted on his head. Someone had taped over it, then used the webbing material to bind his hands so he couldn't remove the tape. Ralston had to laugh at the man's predicament. Then he sobered. What was it like for Westcott to lose that computer contact? Could it be similar to Ralston losing human contact? The P'torra had broken many human fighters using isolation techniques. Was Westcott suffering as a result of his inability to link with the ship's computer?

"Get me out of here, dammit!" raged Westcott. "I will not submit to this indignity!''

"You need rest," said Ralston.

"I need to work!''

"On what?" asked Ralston. "You said you got nothing of importance from the being who claimed to have built the outposts.''

"He did. They are immortal and don't experience death in the manner we do.''

"You need to rest so that you can safely make the shift to Beta 5 for us. We can't leave the others stranded on the planet while we swing in orbit about a gas giant and watch the Jupiter storms.''

"Pah, they mean nothing. There is little on this planet of merit, though they do good theoretical work."

Ralston sized up the mathematician. He phrased his words carefully. "You learned a great deal from the exchange, didn't you? Perhaps not direct knowledge, but some—shall we call them sidebands—crept over, and you saw much you haven't bothered to mention to the rest of us."

"I won't share it. I know how all you other scientists are. If I told you what I learned, you'd demand that I put your name on the research paper. I won't do it. I got this all by myself!"

"What would you do if I told you there wouldn't be any paper, yours or anyone's?"

"Censorship!"

"Death," Ralston said flatly. "We are stranded here. We can't simply shift away. Only you, in direct-connect with the ship's computer, are accurate enough to return us to 5."

"Ching all those fools!" Westcott shouted.

"No," said Ralston, "what'll happen is that the pilot shifts out of the system for a week or two—enough to give him a chance to shift back."

"That's dangerous."

"Possibly fatal," agreed Ralston. "But we have to try—to rescue the others." Ralston didn't like being so overly dramatic. No direct or immediate danger manifested itself to threaten those on Beta 5. Bernssen's observations showed relative quiet in the chaos-induced storms raging on the primary's surface, but Westcott in his self-centered way wouldn't consider anything but his own work as important. Ralston hoped this would shock him into compliance.

"Not fatal. The pilot, even though he is such a clumsy oaf, is competent enough at programming."

"But not as good as you are," said Ralston.

"Of course not."

"We'll be shifting out a small distance within the hour. It'll be necessary to keep you sedated for the entire time."

"My mind! I can't *think* with the chemicals dulling my mind!"

Ralston did the best he could to shrug in the zero-gravity.

"Wait! Damn you, wait! If I get us back to Beta 5, will you promise not to pump me full of drugs?" The desperation in Westcott's voice convinced Ralston that the mathematician would do anything to keep from being sedated.

"Yes."

"Get me out of here. Why waste weeks and weeks starring to some unmapped point when we can go directly to 5? Damned waste of time and effort." Westcott kept grumbling the entire time Ralston pulled him free of his medical webbing. The first thing Westcott did was rip off the tape over his sensor. Ralston saw the relief flood over the man's features.

Westcott's piloting dropped them less than five light seconds from Beta 5.

"Don't let it eat you up inside, Michael," said Leonore Disa. "You knew there would have to be a compromise somewhere along the way. It wasn't that bad a one, all things considered."

"I didn't think it'd mean we'd be stuck in orbit."

"You did, too," she chided. "Using the shuttle as much as we did, had to mean no more jaunts down to Beta 5. Nels' men are finishing up their observations and powering down. Do you think they want to leave their equipment?"

"It is expensive," granted Ralston, "but there's so much to do there that we haven't touched."

"It's given me the chance to complete the reports on the Alphans' diorama."

"I want Nels to do the same. The two of you experienced more in those scenes than I did." Ralston shuddered, thinking of the seizure he'd suffered. Leonore and Bernssen had taken a great chance entering the telepathic dioramas and experiencing their messages, even with the medication to prevent what Westcott called bifurcation.

The one good thing about it was Leonore's accumulation of enough data to finish a detailed and unusual thesis. Too many Ralston saw researched trivial topics. Not this one. Leonore Disa's would make archaeological history. Deservedly.

"He's so busy. You know that, too." Leonore heaved a deep sigh. "Michael, you've got to stop torturing yourself. We can't do it all—*you* can't do it all, even though it's what you want."

He admitted his graduate assistant was right. And that galled him all the more. He'd found not one but two alien cultures touched by the chaos field—and he still knew nothing about the device, its origin, operation, and purpose. Westcott grumbled constantly but appeared to be making some headway in describing mathematically the effects of the field. Given such a beginning, it might be possible to duplicate the chaos device.

Ralston didn't mind Chancellor Salazar and Leonore's father working with the Alphans' telepathic projector. Such a breakthrough meant major advances in treating mental illnesses, teaching at all levels, myriad other applications he only dimly sensed. And the odd glowing tube used by the Betan, which appeared to function without filament or gaseous element, intrigued him, even though this lay beyond his expertise. The lighting tubes had lasted for thousands of years. He and Bernssen had taken several from the base above Beta 7 for study. These would benefit the University financially and give something to society.

It troubled Ralston deeply, thinking how Salazar and the other would use the technology of the chaos device if Westcott successfully unlocked its secrets. Unchecked, it produced instability in stars and eventual novas, epilepsy in humans, catastrophic equipment failure and, from all he'd seen on Beta 5, mutation of the worst kind. Ralston didn't trust Salazar with that kind of power.

He trusted no one with it.

He shuddered when he thought of the uses to which such a weapon might be put by the P'Torra. They devastated entire planets with their biological weapons. Ruin an inhabited planet with chaos? They'd never hesitate. Destroy an entire solar system? The weapon would be launched without a second thought.

"I just wish I could do my job," Ralston said.

"So do it. You don't have to be present on the surface. We've got adequate remote sensing equipment, even if it is starting to show traces of chaotic failure." Leonore chewed her lower lip as she studied her professor. "Michael?"

"I know. We've got to leave soon. That's part of what's worrying me. Even giving those still on the planet anticonvulsives, some are developing symptoms of epilepsy."

"Nels said that a couple are beginning to forget. They start to say something and it's just . . . gone. The chaos effects are erasing their minds."

"I still want to excavate there. The clues we're missing! Think of it, Leonore."

"And the Betan outposts, too. Those are finds that deserve more attention than we've given them."

"We'll never return," Ralston said dejectedly. "This expedition hasn't produced enough to make it worthwhile. Any expedition that has to star longer than a week isn't worth it to the University unless the returns are substancial—or the professor's reputation is such that they feel obligated." Ralston snorted and shook his head. "My reputation's not going to grow with this one."

"It was really Nels' expedition—and Westcott's," she pointed out.

"That makes it even worse," he said. "I can't even mount my own trips. And with what we've discovered, they ought to be *begging* me to form new digs. Think of it, two cultures—one dead, one in peril from the chaos field. We've made huge strides. And just barely started the journey." He folded his arms across his chest and floated away. Leonore started after him, then stopped. She let him simmer in his own misery.

Seventeen days later, they retrieved Nels Bernssen's expedition from the surface of Beta 5 and starred for Novo Terra.

No newsers awaited them when the shuttle touched down on the isolated landing pad. The University of Ilium hadn't even bothered to send transportation to get them back to the campus. Disheartened, Ralston saw to what little he'd salvaged from Beta 5, made sure all his photographic equipment and the precious block circuits recording all he'd done were properly stored for later transport, then called Druanna Thorkkin and asked for a lift.

"Hail the returning heroes, is that it?" she asked.

"Several of us will need rides. Leonore and Nels. Probably Westcott, if you don't mind. If I don't see him safely back in his lab, he'll wander the streets aimlessly for years, hooking into anything using a computer. Kitchen appliances, floaters, streetlamps."

"If I didn't know what a brain-case burnout he was, I'd think you were joking."

"You don't mind?" asked Ralston.

"I'll be out in a half hour. See you then."

Ralston sat on a crate and stared off into the distance, wondering if this actually was the life he wanted to lead.

"Cheer up, Michael," said Leonore. "When you show the chancellor those photos, he'll put in the request for funding. We can get back to the Beta system and finish off those ruins in a proper manner."

"It'll never happen. Salazar might send someone back to strip the Beta dome of anything they can find, but research it? Hardly. With any luck, a few xenosociologists might get a chance to talk with the Betans. But we won't be back in that system again."

"You're such a pessimist. Salazar can't deny the significance of all we've uncovered."

Ralston said nothing more. He knew Leonore might be

trying to dispel his depression. Or she might be that much of a starry-eyed optimist. Either way, he didn't want to dampen her obvious good spirits on having returned safely to Novo Terra.

When Druanna came to take them back to campus, Ralston pumped her for any gossip. He saw it as a good excuse not to have to talk about the expedition.

"Dr. Ralston, we've gone over your findings. To say that you've exhibited shoddy technique is an understatement."

"Chancellor Salazar," Ralston answered, knowing how those who'd endured the Spanish Inquisition had felt just prior to the physical torture. Ralston cleared his throat and started again. "Dr. Salazar, my techniques may have lacked scientific rigor but they were necessary, under the circumstances."

"This lighting element seems interesting," another on the Committee for Academics said. "We might be able to exploit such technology to University advantage."

"The winds of chaos are blowing through the Beta system," Ralston said, ignoring the comment. "Weather patterns are disrupted. Mutations of an awful variety occur. Dr. Bernssen has already related the instability in this system's star. It will go nova soon."

"Yes, we've discussed his work. Sound technique, good results."

"I discovered an alien race," Ralston said, frustrated. No matter what he said, Salazar and the others on the committee ignored him. "They require immediate aid. Their sun's going to explode and destroy them if we don't do something."

"There's nothing we can do about this nova business," said Salazar.

"Evacuation! Aid to build ships. The Betans need to leave!"

"And go where, Dr. Ralston?" asked Salazar. "Here? I am sure they'd enjoy an oxygen atmosphere. Your report

states that they are ammonia and methane breathers.''
Salazar ran his fingers over a console and read parts of
Ralston's report on the monitor. "Yes, and high-pressure
beings, too."

"It's their lighting element you're salivating over."

"You forget yourself, Doctor," snapped Salazar.

"You're not going to help the Betans? You're going to
sit by and allow an entire race to be snuffed out in a
nova?"

"Such aid is beyond the scope of the University of
Ilium," Salazar said pointedly. "A report will be for-
warded to the government, but their decision is likely to be
one of neutrality. What do we know of these creatures?"

"They're intelligent and have a complex society. They
established colonies on another planet in their system.
They have advanced communications capability. They—"

"Irrelevant, Dr. Ralston. It pains me to say this, but
intelligent races litter the starways." Salazar made a gesture of distaste. "Several insist on educating their young at
our school."

"You won't have to worry about the Betans," Ralston
said nastily. "They'll be snuffed out in less time than it
takes to file an application for admission."

"Good. Now that the matter is settled, we can continue
to other points barely touched upon in your report."

Ralston sat in stunned silence. Salazar had dismissed an
entire race with that simple statement. It mattered nothing
to him that the Betans would die. Ralston barely compre-
hended how the Betans themselves could be indifferent to
their fate. Not only were they alien, their body structures
and chemistry were alien in the extreme. The one who'd
called himself an aberrant implied that they were immortal, that they had no natural enemies or need to fight for
sustenance. Ralston understood such a race wouldn't think
like a human.

But what race did Salazar come from? Ralston sat and
listened in silence as the Committee on Academics concluded their meeting. Salazar was human. Maybe all too

human in the way he wrapped himself in his work to the extent of forgetting his humanity.

". . . in conclusion, we will again review Dr. Ralston's work in, hmm, one month. At that time we shall make recommendations for change in his field techniques and ways to improve the overall quality of his work. Dismissed, Dr. Ralston."

Michael Ralston stood without a word. In a daze, he left the meeting room. Of all those present, only he realized that Chancellor Salazar, by deciding on inaction, had killed an entire race.

Even worse, Ralston worried about the chaos field. It still traveled from star to star, leaving behind its random legacy of confusion and death. The Alphans had died. The Betans were next. How many others had there been? How many more would there be?

Chancellor Salazar might not care, but Ralston did.

SIXTEEN

"I'VE FAILED," RALSTON told Leonore Disa. "Every time I get in the same room with Salazar, I start losing my temper. I can't help it. It's just the way that man strikes me."

"It didn't sound that bad," Leonore said without much conviction.

"Salazar is holding another hearing in a month or two and will decide then what to do about me. He suggested I needed some remedial work. Sloppy archaeology, he called the expedition. And it was. Dammit, he's right. That makes me madder than anything else!"

"The time pressure prevented us from doing more than we did. He ought to know that. So should you," she said, brushing back her short brown hair and peering up at him. "You might be an archaeology professor but that doesn't make you a god."

"It doesn't make me good at politics, either," said Ralston. "Salazar refuses to listen to me about the importance of finding the chaos field. We've got to track it, go to it, investigate it. This is the ultimate artifact, Leonore. Think. A device that challenges the basic parameters of the universe itself. What race designed it? Why? Did it get away from them or was it intentionally sent on its course? Why this particular trajectory? The questions!"

"I know, I know, Michael. But just because Salazar doesn't agree that it's worth investigating doesn't mean you don't have some allies. Nels is at a seminar at the University of Novo Terra. Interest is incredible among the astrophysicists. They see the chaos field as an opportunity of a lifetime."

"It is!"

"They don't care if it's natural or constructed, though."

"It's artificial. It had to be. I feel it in my bones."

"Very scientific," Leonore said, laughing. She reached out and lightly touched his arm. "But I agree. Look, I'm flying over to Novo City to meet Nels. Want to come?"

He shook his head. He had no business being with them.

"Suit yourself. We'll be back before midnight. Nels might want to talk to you then about the seminar's outcome. Will you be at home?"

"Try my office. I've got a hundred years worth of data to sort before I can get down and do any real thinking about what it all means."

"Your office. Midnight. Bye." With that, Leonore took off, almost skipping with happiness.

Ralston wished he could share even a gram of that cheerfulness. But he couldn't. All the expedition had done for him was to reinforce his opinions. Opinions—nothing more.

Ralston found himself walking across the quiet campus toward Westcott's laboratory. He didn't want to confront the mathematician, but he found this less disagreeable than being alone. Druanna Thorkkin had classes for the rest of the afternoon and into the early evening, and he had no one else to occupy his time or take his mind off his considerable concerns.

Ralston paused at the door into Westcott's lab, took a deep breath, knocked and went in, eyes closed. He remembered all too vividly the last time he'd barged in. Slowly, Ralston opened his eyes. Again he spun through space, odd music ringing in his ears. Whatever there was about this tri-dee screen and the musical patterns that soothed Westcott, it only disoriented Ralston.

"Westcott?" he called softly. Through the darkness he saw the mathematician hunched over the computer console. The IR sensor on his head blazed a pure red light. A blink, then solid beaming again. Whatever held Westcott's attention, he used the mind-computer link to its fullest capacity.

"Ralston!" Westcott spun and had a smile as broad as any Ralston had ever seen. "I've done it. This is the most elegant work I have ever done!"

"What's that? Something with your quantum gravity theory?"

"That? No, no, why bother with that? I'm talking about the chaos equations. I've found a solution."

Ralston felt as if he'd stepped into an empty elevator shaft and plummeted for the core of the planet. Should he kill Westcott? The man was unique on the campus. No one else could have derived the solution to such complex mathematical structures. Ralston didn't want the University— and Salazar—in possession of such a potent secret.

Weapons? Salazar would have no qualms about licensing the technology that would come from the theoretical solution to the highest bidder. Ralston wouldn't tolerate the P'torra ever obtaining the secret. To prevent the misuse, Ralston would gladly kill Westcott.

"It's not a general solution, but that'll come. Oh, yes, that'll follow. I used a simplified set of assumptions to begin with, then predicted radioactive decay in uranium. I used one of deCastro's fourteen atom specimens, that being the smallest he had on hand. I applied the boundary conditions, determined which of the fourteen atoms would show decay—and it did!"

"You predicted only one decay?"

"I predicted seventy-four consecutive decays. I need a larger universe, a larger sample. DeCastro said he could manufacture a thirty-atom sample for me. I see no trouble in predicting the decay there, either."

"I didn't think the chaos field caused noticeable radioactive decay."

"The residual effects can't cause decay because of reversal, but my equations can *predict*. The other effects of the field—the weather and component failure and the rest—will fall into place when I have a better handle on the system."

"So this is only a small step?"

"Small, but significant." Westcott cackled and rubbed his hands together. "I'll go down in history with Gauss and Lobatchevsky and Minkowsky. When I find a general solution to the system, *then* they'll notice me!"

Ralston blinked in surprise. He'd never heard Westcott talk in such a fashion before. Fame seemed an unlikely pursuit for the mathematician, yet the need must well from deep within him, driving him onward.

"It's only a simple set of nonlinear equations, but I've learned so much. The Betan gave me so much. Just knowing the chaos field was artificial told me so much."

"It is!" Ralston sank to the floor, sitting cross-legged and staring at Westcott. "Why didn't you tell me before?"

"You knew it." Westcott frowned. "Or you seemed to know. The observations made by the Betans—or the aberrant one with curiosity—verified it. There were large metallic projections on the body that radiated in the ultraviolet. The Betan's instruments weren't good enough to pick up the exact frequencies, but I don't think that matters. No, not at all, not at all." Westcott began chuckling again.

"Why not?" Ralston asked, intrigued in spite of himself. He ought to be angry at the mathematician for withholding this from him for purely selfish reasons, but the sheer impact of the information robbed him of any emotion other than interest.

"It is not a physical device in the strict sense, in the way we'd mean. This is a conceptual machine."

"I don't understand."

"I don't either, not exactly. But I will. The mathematics is so intricate, so elegant!"

"We need to study it in ways other than just documenting its effects," said Ralston, more to himself than to Westcott. "Direct observation. If there are artificial structures, these might tell us something of the race that built it."

Ralston fell into deep depression at the thought of being forced to remain at the University of Ilium and never again go starring. Salazar wouldn't authorize any expedition headed by Ralston—ever. Ralston had ridden along on Nels Bernssen's good luck to excavate in the Beta system, but he couldn't count on the physicist's and his own interests to converge again in the future.

But to examine such a relic!

"I need to see it," said Westcott. "Nothing else will suffice. If it is more concept than physical, only by witnessing it in action can I get a handle on the mathematics involved. Boundary conditions are everything in the chaos equations. Parameters varying by infinitesimals produce radical changes."

Ralston smiled. He might not be able to mount the needed expedition, but Westcott could. Ralston chuckled. He had chided Bernssen about astronomy becoming an experimental science. What would the academic community say about pure mathematics similarly changing?

"Are you interested in tracking the chaos device down?" Ralston asked, trying to keep the eagerness from his voice.

"I know the trajectory with some exactitude. Simple calculations give me the volume of space where it is likely to be. Yes, definitely, I must go."

"You arrange the funding, I'll put together the equipment."

"Equipment? I don't need much. A few cameras. A spectroscope, possibly. Definitely I need monitoring of the local gravity fields to determine the proper tensor strength. But a single ship and one or two people to assist will be sufficient. I don't want more. Too confusing and distracting for me."

"You don't want to be bothered by details. I'll take care of that in exchange for the chance to go along."

"Don't bother with him," came Leonore's voice. She and Nels Bernssen walked into Westcott's lab. "Nels has a better proposition."

Ralston dared to hope again.

He turned to see Leonore and Bernssen in the doorway. "You weren't in your office so we decided to stop here," said the woman. "Nels got back early, saving me a trip. Go on, Nels, tell him."

"I've just finished one of the most incredible meetings of my life," the physicist said. "Can't believe it, even now. They almost thrust money at me and begged me to take it. The Bernssen Condition has moved up from theory to reality in most of their minds—and I haven't even written the definitive paper yet!"

"Trivial," said Westcott, annoyed at the crowd in his laboratory. "Compared to the solution of the chaos equations, this is nothing."

"You might be right," said Leonore, "but Nels is already planning an expedition to follow the chaos device. He needs measurements to determine the forces that alter the nuclear chain in stars. With this, he might be able to formulate a more accurate theory of conditions inside a normal star."

"I—" began Ralston.

"We can go, Michael," said Leonore. "We might not have much of a role to play with so many physicists running loose, but we can go."

"I'll resign my position with the University, if necessary," said Ralston. "I know the discovery of the century—of all time!—when I see it."

"See what I meant, Nels?" the woman said. "I told you he'd be hard to convince."

Ralston didn't care who commanded the expedition. The knowledge this would yield would be priceless, beyond money, beyond even ego. He had to share in the exploration process, not for fame or glory, but for the *need* to know. No other archaeological discovery in history was as significant—or deadly.

He was through following the wake of destruction left by the chaos device. The time had come to study it directly.

"When do we leave?" Michael Ralston asked.